Who was *this strange woman?*

Robin wasn't about to touch her face. Not after shaking Yaga's hand. The witch's palm was as slimy as an eel.

"So how long have you been here, Yaga?" Robin's mother asked.

"Hundreds of years," Yaga answered, biting off another piece of peanut brittle.

Robin's mother chuckled. "I mean, how long has the orchard been open?"

"Today," Yaga answered. "It's our grand opening. That's why everything is free."

"That's what we thought," Robin's mother told her. "Only we didn't see any announcement in the paper this morning."

Yaga chuckled. "We don't like to advertise," she said. "We have plenty of *other* ways to get customers . . ."

D0804139

DEADTIME STORIES™

Invasion of the Appleheads

A. G. Cascone

Troll

*For Mary and John,
for being there . . . when the rest
of the world turned into appleheads.*

If you purchased this book without a cover, you should be aware that this book is stolen property. It was reported as "unsold and destroyed" to the publisher, and neither the author nor the publisher has received any payment for this "stripped book."

Copyright © 1996 by Annette Cascone and Gina Cascone.

Cover art copyright © 1996 by Broeck Steadman.

Published by Troll Communications L.L.C.

Deadtime Stories is a trademark of Annette Cascone and Gina Cascone.

Appleheads carved by Debbie, Carousel Doll Shoppe.

All rights reserved. No part of this book may be reproduced or utilized in any form or by any means, electronic or mechanical, including photocopying, recording, or by any information storage and retrieval system, without written permission from the publisher.

Printed in the United States of America.

10 9 8 7 6 5 4 3 2 1

CHAPTER 1

Robin Carter was sure the torture would never end. She had to struggle to hold back the scream in her throat. Because she knew that if she screamed, things would only get worse.

That is, if things *could* get worse.

"Isn't this fun, kids?" Robin's mother asked cheerily.

No! Robin wanted to yell at the top of her lungs. *This is not fun! This is the worst possible way to spend a day!*

It was a beautiful, sunny Sunday. It was also the day before Halloween. That's what made things really bad.

Robin wanted to be home putting the finishing touches on her Halloween costume and getting ready for the big parade. The Halloween parade was the biggest event in Appleton. All of the kids in Robin's school were excited about it.

Robin was excited about it too, especially since she'd been invited to a party after the parade by Christine Baker, the most popular girl in her class. Starting the fifth grade in a new school had been hard enough, but making new friends had been even harder.

Unfortunately, Robin wasn't at home right now working on her Halloween costume. Because Robin was crammed into the backseat of the car with her eleven-year-old brother, Andy, who didn't want to be driving around Appleton any more than she did. All because their parents had insisted they spend the day together visiting the town's historical sights.

"Are we going to stop soon?" Andy moaned.

"Yes," Mrs. Carter answered. "We're almost there."

"Almost where?" Robin whispered to her brother. "What stupid thing are we going to have to look at next?"

"Probably the biggest rock in Appleton," Andy whispered back.

They both snickered.

Robin and her family had moved to Appleton just a few months before. They used to live in the city, but Robin's parents had decided that a small town would be a much better place for them to grow up.

Appleton *was* a small town. A small, *creepy* town, in Robin's opinion. It had been founded in the 1600s, and most of it still looked three hundred years old. Even the neighborhood Robin and her family lived in looked like a page from a history book.

Traveling through Appleton was like driving through a time warp. Except for the mall, there was nothing modern looking at all.

Robin hated it.

But her parents adored it. They thought Appleton was the greatest place in the universe.

The morning before, Robin's mother had picked up a little guidebook at the library that told about all the historical sights in their new town. Before the day was over, they were going to visit every single one of them.

"I can't believe we spent twenty minutes looking at a stupid piece of cement," Robin complained to Andy.

Even though Robin had whispered, her mother heard her. "What piece of cement?" she asked.

"The one that said 'George Washington crossed here,'" Robin answered. "What was so interesting about that?"

"That was very interesting," Mr. Carter answered. "It was the route that Washington took on his way to an important battle of the Revolution," he started to explain. "He—"

"I know. I know." Robin stopped her father. She couldn't stand to hear the story again. History was just about her least favorite subject in the world.

"So what are we going to see next?" Andy asked, sounding as impatient as Robin felt.

"The next stop is the Appleton Orchard," Mrs. Carter said, checking the guidebook.

Robin and Andy rolled their eyes.

"Do you want to hear what the guidebook says about it?" their mother asked.

"Nooooooo!" Robin and Andy answered at the same time.

"Of course we do," Mr. Carter said, shooting Robin and Andy a scolding look over his shoulder.

"I think you kids are really going to like this," their mother told them.

That was what she'd been promising all day. It hadn't been true yet.

"'The Appleton Orchard was originally owned by a woman who was accused of being a witch,'" Mrs. Carter read.

"Sounds pretty spooky, kids," Mr. Carter chimed in, trying to stir up their interest.

"Listen to this." Their mother continued to read. "'The townspeople believed that the witch was putting some kind of magic potion into her apples, a potion that turned all the children of Appleton into zombies. On Halloween Night, three hundred years ago, the angry parents burned the orchard to the ground.'"

"Pretty cool!" Andy said.

Robin agreed the story was cool, but she still wasn't sure about going there. "If the orchard was burned to the ground, what is there to see?" she pointed out.

"The book says that the witch's house is still standing," her mother told her. "It's the oldest house in Appleton. And it wasn't even damaged in the fire."

Who wanted to see another stupid old house? Robin slumped against the car door. Things *had* gotten worse.

"Look at that," Mr. Carter said a second later as the orchard came into view.

A banner stretched across the road. It read, "Welcome to Appleton Orchard!"

There were hand-painted signs posted every few feet. "Free Candy Apples!" "Free Apple Cider!" "Free Haunted Hayrides!"

"I thought this place was supposed to be deserted," Robin said.

"Well, it certainly looks full of life today," her father replied as he drove toward the huge iron gates that led into the orchard. "Maybe someone has taken over the place. This looks like some kind of grand opening celebration."

"That's funny," Mrs. Carter chimed in. "I didn't see anything about it in the paper this morning. If I had, we could have skipped the sightseeing tour and spent the day here."

Robin shot her brother a look. Too bad there hadn't been anything in the paper. The orchard sounded a *little* more interesting than anything else they'd seen so far. Maybe they could have been spared a whole day of torture.

"Well, we're here now," Mr. Carter said, turning through the gates. "And we've still got a couple of good hours before it gets dark."

As they entered the grounds, Robin felt something strange. Something that made her shiver. It was as if she'd passed through some kind of invisible wall, or like diving into a pool and breaking through the surface of the water. And it happened just as quickly.

Strangely, outside the gates, the trees were turning colors and losing their leaves, but inside the gates, the apple trees were in full bloom—green and loaded with fruit.

Robin turned around in her seat to look back at the gates.

Something else was wrong. But it took Robin a minute to figure out what it was.

Outside the gates, where the leaves on the trees were dying, it was a beautiful, sunny day. But inside the gates, where everything blossomed, it was dark and dreary.

Robin shivered again. "Creepy," she said, talking to herself.

"What's creepy?" her mother asked.

"The trees," Robin answered. "How come they've still got apples?"

"Maybe the apple season is longer out here in the country," her mother said.

"But look how dark it is in here," Robin pointed out.

Her father laughed. "Of course it's dark," he said. "We're in the shadow of all these trees."

Robin caught a glimpse of the sky above the trees. It was steely gray, with no sunshine at all.

But before Robin could point that out to her family, the words stuck in her throat as a hideous creature stepped out from between the apple trees that lined the drive. Its head was swollen, and the green, putrid skin that covered its face was rotting right off its skull. Bloodshot eyeballs hung from their sockets. And a blood-covered ax stuck out of its chest.

"Look!" Mrs. Carter exclaimed as another grotesque creature appeared ahead of them. "Everyone is dressed up for Halloween!"

Robin took a good look at the creature with the ax in its chest. If that was a costume, it was very, very good.

"This is excellent!" Andy said. "I definitely want to go on the haunted hayride."

"Didn't I tell you this would be fun?" Mrs. Carter said.

They pulled into the parking lot under a giant old shade tree where several other cars were already parked. But there were no other people in the parking lot. Just the biggest, creepiest-looking scarecrow on a pole that Robin had ever seen.

Its head was the size of a basketball, and it was covered with a dirty white sheet that was tied around its neck with a thick, heavy rope dangling to the ground like a leash. Its face was painted onto the sheet.

The second her father parked the car, the creature started to move!

Robin let out a loud, startled cry.

So did her mother.

"It's all right," Robin's father assured them. "It's just someone dressed up in a Halloween costume."

The giant creature climbed down from its pole and started clomping its way toward them, flailing its arms and moaning. It looked like Frankenstein's monster dressed up as a scarecrow.

No one made a move to get out of the car.

"If he's trying to scare us away, he's doing a pretty

good job," Robin's mother chuckled nervously.

The scarecrow fell onto the hood of the car, moaning and groaning even louder than before.

"Let's get out of here!" Robin cried.

But it was too late.

Within seconds, the car was surrounded by cackling witches and blood-covered ghouls.

And Robin had the horrible feeling that they weren't just people in Halloween costumes.

CHAPTER 2

"Oooooooooo-WAAAAAAAAY!" the scarecrow moaned, peering through the windshield at them. *"OOOOOOOO-WAAAAAAAAY!"*

Robin could see the scarecrow's beady black eyes glaring at them from behind the sheet with his painted-on face. His body was so huge and bulky, it covered the entire hood of the car.

Robin's heart pounded against her chest even harder than the scarecrow's massive fists were pounding the glass.

"Do something, Dad!" Robin yelled.

"Everybody just stay calm," Mr. Carter said, sounding anything *but* calm. "I'm sure he's just acting scary for Halloween."

"Then he's a really good actor!" Robin shot back.

"'Cause he's scaring me half to death!"

"OOOOOOOOOOO-WAAAAAAAAAY!" the scarecrow kept moaning.

"What in the world is he saying?" Mrs. Carter said. She sounded pretty scared herself.

"I don't know," Mr. Carter answered, shooting Mrs. Carter a worried look.

Robin didn't want to know. She just wanted to get out of there. Fast!

"Back up, Dad!" Robin cried.

"He can't back up!" Andy said. "He'll run over all those ghouls on our trunk!"

The ghouls weren't just climbing on the trunk. They were banging on the windows. And hanging off the roof.

Just then another voice screeched through the air.

"OOOOOOOO-WEN!" the voice bellowed. "Get away from that car before I turn you into a tongueless little newt! All of you! Away from the car!"

The wrinkled old woman who raced toward the car looked even more horrible than she sounded. She was dressed in a witch's costume. But Robin didn't think she had on any makeup at all. Her shriveled old skin really was a sickly green color. And the hairy wart hanging from the end of her nose wasn't glued on.

"Oh, look." Mrs. Carter relaxed as the witch swatted the ghouls with her broom. "They're just putting on a little show for us," she said.

"Get away from the car, Owen," the gnarled old woman growled. Then she grabbed the rope hanging from the scarecrow's neck and gave it a tug. "Keep it up, and I'll lock you back in the dungeon!"

The scarecrow quickly climbed down from the hood. He was shaking and cowering. Robin had the feeling he really was afraid of the witch.

"Bad Owen," the witch hollered, waving her gnarled finger in front of his face. "Bad, bad Owen."

"Owen?" Andy rolled his eyes. "The scarecrow's name is Owen?"

"He looks more like Dr. Frankenstein's monster to me," Robin said.

Mrs. Carter laughed. "You see?" she said. "Everything is fine!"

"Welcome to Appleton Orchard!" The witch cackled as she pressed her hairy wart nose up against Robin's window. "Come out, dear," she said, beckoning Robin with a crooked finger. Then she reached into her pocket and pulled out a huge clump of peanut brittle. "I have lots of goodies for you!"

CHAPTER 3

Robin shot her parents a look that said, *Please don't make me get out of this car!* But her parents were already climbing out themselves.

"Don't be afraid," the witch said as she pulled open Robin's door. "We're just having fun. Aren't we, Owen?"

The scarecrow let out a nervous moan as the witch bit off a piece of the peanut brittle she held in her twisted fingers.

Robin drew back at the sight of the gooey brown gunk swishing around the witch's stained yellow teeth.

"That's one heck of a welcoming committee you've got there," Mr. Carter said as he headed toward the witch.

"It sure is," Mrs. Carter agreed. "For a second, you even had *us* fooled."

"I hope we didn't scare you too badly," the witch said. "Our scarecrow loves Halloween. And he loves trying to scare all the children away. Don't you, Owen?" she growled.

Owen didn't answer. He just lowered his head as if he were ashamed.

"Don't mind him," the witch said. She winked at Andy. "The cat bit off Owen's tongue when he was just a little boy. And she swallowed it right up!"

Robin and Andy exchanged nervous glances as the witch started to cackle.

"I'm Yaga," she said, sticking out her hand to Robin. "And you're my next victim."

Yaga had the worst breath Robin had ever smelled. It was so foul, Robin wanted to cover her nose. Only she wasn't about to touch her face. Not after shaking Yaga's hand. The witch's palm was as slimy as an eel.

"So how long have you been here, Yaga?" Mrs. Carter asked.

"Hundreds of years," Yaga answered, biting off another piece of peanut brittle.

Robin's mother laughed. "I mean, how long has the orchard been open?"

"Today," Yaga answered. "It's our grand opening. That's why everything is free."

"That's what we thought," Mrs. Carter told her. "But we didn't see any announcement in the paper this morning."

Yaga chuckled. "We don't like to advertise," she said. "We have plenty of *other* ways to get customers."

Just then another old witch headed toward them, carrying a tray loaded with candy apples and steaming hot cups.

"Can Drusila and I offer you some hot apple cider and sweet candy apples before you set off on the scariest hayride of your lives?" Yaga asked.

"I'd love some hot apple cider," Mrs. Carter said.

"Me too," added Mr. Carter.

"I brewed it myself," Yaga said, handing over the cups. "It does wonders for your head."

Mrs. Carter looked at Yaga, confused.

Yaga's lips twisted into a ghoulish grin. "It clears the sinuses," she said.

"Oh." Mrs. Carter nodded politely, then took a sip. "Mmmm . . . it's absolutely delicious."

"How about some candy apples for you two?" Drusila, the other witch, asked Robin and Andy. She smiled, exposing her four rotten teeth.

"I'd like one," Andy said, reaching for an apple.

"And you, my little pretty?" Drusila leered at Robin.

"Sure," Robin said, taking one. "Thanks."

Drusila kept right on leering. "You have beautiful eyes," she told Robin. "Look how green and full of life they are!" Drusila seemed so excited by Robin's eyes that she was actually snorting with glee.

"They *are* full of life, aren't they?" Yaga grinned, leering at Robin too.

Yaga's stare sent shivers racing across Robin's flesh. Yaga's eyes were the creepiest part of her. The left one was grayer than charcoal, but the right one was so blue and sparkling, it looked like crystal. Robin couldn't turn away from her hypnotic stare.

It was as if Yaga's eyes were trying to suck the life right out of her.

"Robin has her mother's eyes," Mr. Carter said, pulling Yaga's attention away from Robin.

"She does at that," Yaga agreed, peering at Mrs. Carter. "Your eyes are as green as emeralds too. They're enticing," she told Mrs. Carter.

"Thank you." Mrs. Carter acknowledged the compliment. Then she glanced at the house that stood at the far side of the parking lot. "After the hayride, I'd love to go inside the house. I understand it's the oldest house in Appleton."

Robin looked at the rickety old building. The huge gray stone walls were cracking and crumbling, and the wooden steps that led up to the door were rotting away. Thick, heavy grime covered the windows, and the shutters were hanging half off. Robin couldn't understand why in the world her mother would want to go in there. It didn't even look safe.

"Yes." Yaga smiled her ugly smile. "Of course you'll see the house. Our little gift shop is inside. That's where everyone ends up. But first, you must go on the hayride." Yaga clapped her hands loudly. "Owen!" she bellowed. "Prepare the next cart!"

"Oh, no," Andy whispered to Robin. "Not Owen."

Robin didn't want to get in a cart with Owen either. But

it didn't look like they had a choice. In the far distance, Robin now saw that the only other cart was already loaded with another set of parents and their two kids. Robin had never seen so much red hair in her life. It looked like a carriage full of rooster heads.

"Just go on over to the barn," Yaga said. "Owen will take real good care of you folks."

"Thanks, Yaga," Mr. Carter said. "I haven't been on a hayride in years. This is going to be great!"

Mrs. Carter giggled. "A *haunted* hayride," she reminded Mr. Carter. "Good thing you'll be with me," she added, taking his hand. "In case I get scared."

"I'll be listening for your screams." Yaga laughed.

Mr. and Mrs. Carter grinned as they raced for the barn.

Robin couldn't believe how goofy her parents were acting. It was almost like *they* were the kids and she and Andy were the adults.

"OOOO-BAAAACK," Owen grunted as they reached the cart.

"Okay," Mr. Carter agreed. "I'll go in the back." He climbed up into the cart.

Mrs. Carter got in next.

"Oooo-baaaack," Mr. Carter said, imitating Owen with a chuckle. "That's such a great monster voice."

Mrs. Carter giggled again as she sat down next to her husband.

Owen just moaned.

Andy climbed in next and sat opposite his parents. Robin plunked herself down alongside Andy as Owen turned around and settled into the driver's seat. Then he snapped the reins hard, and the horses started to pull the cart forward.

"Here we go!" Mrs. Carter exclaimed.

"Isn't this neat?" Mr. Carter said, taking a sip of his cider.

The cart headed down the dusty old path toward the twisted apple trees. There were so many trees up ahead, it looked more like a forest than an orchard.

Robin unwrapped the candy apple Drusila had given her as she settled in for the ride. So far the orchard had been more interesting than she'd expected, but she still wanted to go home to prepare for Halloween. With any luck, the ride would be over by the time she finished her apple.

Robin lifted the apple to her mouth and bit off a huge, juicy chunk. The second the apple hit Robin's tongue, the sugary, sweet taste dissolved into something bitter and foul—and sickeningly slimy!

Robin's stomach rose up to her throat. The chunk of gunk in her mouth was moving! Robin could feel something squiggling across her tongue!

CHAPTER 4

"A worm!" Robin spit out the piece of apple in her mouth. "There's a worm in my candy apple!" she shrieked.

"Let me see," Andy said.

Robin kept right on spitting as she shoved her candy apple under Andy's nose.

Sure enough, there was a rotten brown spot right where she'd bitten into the apple. In the center was a little hole where half a worm was squiggling around.

"Gross!" Andy said, pushing Robin's apple away from his face.

"Yuk! Yuk! Yuk!" Robin hurled the apple over the side of the cart as hard as she could. Then she grabbed a handful of tissues from her jacket pocket and started wiping her tongue with them. She'd never be able to get the taste of worm out of her mouth.

"Calm down, Robin," her mother said. "I know it's awful to find a worm in your apple. But it's not going to kill you. Forget about it."

Easy for her to say! Robin thought. *She isn't the one who bit into a worm!*

Andy just sat there looking at his own candy apple.

"I wouldn't eat that if I were you," Robin told him.

Andy nodded. Then he pitched his candy apple out of the cart too. "Some haunted hayride," he said. "So far all we've gotten is rotten candy apples."

"For real," Robin agreed. "It was scarier in the parking lot."

As the cart moved ahead, Robin could see a bunch of kids out in the orchards picking apples. Some of them went to her school.

"Mark," Robin called out to one of the boys she recognized. He was up on a ladder picking apples from a tree.

Only he didn't answer.

"Hey, Mark," she called out again, a little bit louder this time. "What are you doing here?"

He still didn't answer. He didn't even look her way. He just kept picking apples, moving his arms up and down like a robot.

"Mark!" she shouted as the cart passed right by him. Nothing.

"Who's that?" Andy teased her. "Your boyfriend?"

"No," Robin answered. "He's just a kid from school."

"He seems like a real jerk," Andy said.

"He's not a jerk," Robin said. Actually, Mark was one of the nicest kids in her class. He had even shown her around on the first day of school. Robin couldn't understand why he was being so rude to her all of a sudden, acting as if she wasn't even there. It was like he was in a trance.

Robin looked around at the other kids picking apples. All of them seemed to be in some kind of trance. They were all moving like robots.

Robin stared at one of the boys near Mark, who seemed to be staring back at her. But his eyes were totally vacant, as if the life had been sucked out of them.

Suddenly Robin remembered what her mother had read about the orchard. It used to be owned by a witch who used apples to turn all the children of Appleton into . . .

"Zombies!" Robin gasped.

"What?" Andy said.

"All those kids," Robin murmured. She could feel the color drain out of her face.

"What are you talking about?" her mother asked.

"Just look around," Robin said. "Those kids are moving like robots, and their eyes are glassy and blank."

But her mother never got the chance to look. Because suddenly, everything around them disappeared in a poof of smoke.

CHAPTER 5

"What's going on?" Robin screamed in terror. "Where are we?"

Robin couldn't see a thing. She couldn't even see her own hand in front of her face.

"I don't like this one bit." Andy's voice came from beside her.

Deep laughter rose from the dense mist that surrounded them.

"Dad?" Robin cried. "Mom?"

Something touched Robin's knee. She jumped back as she let out another scream.

"It's okay." Her father's voice came from across the cart. "It's just me." His hand patted her arm.

"Dad, I can't see you," Andy said nervously. "I can't see *anything!*"

"That's because we're in thick fog," Mrs. Carter's voice explained.

"How can we be in fog?" Robin asked. "It was a beautiful, sunny day before we came to this creepy orchard."

"Maybe they set up a fog machine out here," her father answered. "This must be the haunted part of our hayride. Everybody get ready to be scared."

Robin was already scared. And it didn't help her nerves one bit when her mother let out a heavy sigh.

"Oh, my goodness." Mrs. Carter sounded very strange. Her voice seemed small and faraway. "All of a sudden, I don't feel very well."

"Neither do I," Robin's father said. His voice sounded just as odd. Tiny. Squeaky even.

"What's wrong?" Robin asked.

There was no answer.

"Mom?" Robin said.

Her mother didn't answer.

"Dad?"

He didn't answer either.

"Stop trying to scare us," Andy ordered.

"Yeah," Robin agreed. "You guys are not funny."

There was no reply.

"Robin!" Andy yelped. "What's going on?"

"I don't know," Robin answered. "Maybe Owen can tell us."

But before Robin could yell to the giant scarecrow, the cart jerked to a stop. Then Robin heard voices. Strange, eerie, whispering voices.

What the heck is going on now? Robin wondered.

"Andy?" Robin strained to see her brother through the fog. "Are you okay?"

"Yeah," he answered. Only he didn't sound okay.

Then something touched her arm. At first, Robin thought it was Andy. But it wasn't Andy at all!

Something was wrapping itself around Robin's arm like a snake. And it was squeezing so tightly, Robin's arm started to tingle with numbness.

Robin reached over to pull at it with her free hand.

As soon as she touched it, she realized that it wasn't a snake. It felt like a tree branch or a vine. And it was twisted around her flesh like a thick wooden rope.

"Let go of me!" Robin cried as she struggled to pull it away. But just as she started to tug, something grabbed her free hand and yanked *it* away instead.

Robin started to scream.

Her arms were being pulled in two different directions! She was sure that her whole body was going to be ripped right in two.

"Andy!" she yelled. "Help me!"

"I can't," Andy screamed back. "Something scratchy's grabbing my arms! It won't let go!"

Something cold and wet pressed down hard on the back of Robin's hand. It lasted only a second, and then the vines started unwrapping themselves from her arms. Suddenly Robin was free.

The cart jerked forward quickly. They were moving again.

"Andy?" Robin cried in a panic. "Are you still here?"

Andy didn't have to answer Robin's question because as soon as she finished asking it, the fog started to lift and Robin could see him clearly. He was sitting next to her, trembling with fear.

"It's okay," Robin said, as much to herself as to Andy. Only it wasn't okay.

Robin and Andy had come out of the fog. But their parents were gone!

CHAPTER 6

"Mom?" Robin yelled as loud as she could. "Dad? Where are you?"

There was no answer.

Robin looked back at the fog that lay on the ground like a giant white cloud. Her parents were somewhere in that mist. She was sure of it. Their disappearing act was probably a joke they were trying to play to make the hayride *really* scary.

"Hey, Owen," Andy screamed. "You've got to stop this cart! Our parents are gone!"

Owen paid no attention to Andy. He just kept on driving.

Robin moved closer to Owen and tapped him on the shoulder. "Excuse me," she said loudly.

Owen turned around and fixed his dark, beady eyes

on Robin. He was breathing heavily. This was not a friendly scarecrow.

"Something happened to our parents!" Robin shouted at him. "You have to stop this cart!"

Robin could tell by the way Owen was glaring at her that he knew exactly what had happened. And she had the awful feeling that he wasn't going to help them either. But she wasn't about to give up.

"Our parents are lost in the fog. We have to go back and find them," she insisted.

Owen opened his mouth and let out a groan, along with a puff of horrible breath that Robin could actually see in the chilly air. Then he turned back around and continued driving the cart forward, faster than before.

"I think we should jump off and go look for them ourselves," Andy said. He looked as if he were about ready to do just that.

Robin grabbed the back of his jacket. "We can't do that," she said. "What if we end up lost in the fog too? We're just going to have to wait until we get back to the parking lot and ask someone there to help us."

"Like who?" Andy asked. "Those creepy-looking ghouls?"

"They're just people in Halloween costumes," Robin reminded him. At least she *hoped* they were.

Besides, there was a much bigger problem.

"Uh-oh," Andy said. "It doesn't look like we're going back to the parking lot."

"What are you talking about?" Robin asked.

Andy pointed.

Along the path up ahead of them, another cart had stopped beside an old, run-down shack. The door of the shack was chained up and locked. The windows were covered with thick iron bars, like a prison.

There were two kids in the cart ahead of them. Robin recognized them right away.

"Andy," she gasped. "It's those two redheaded kids. The ones who got on the hayride just before we did."

They were dull and sleepy-looking, like the kids Robin had seen in the orchard.

"Their parents are gone too!" Andy cried.

Robin watched in horror as the driver up ahead lifted the two zombielike children out of the cart. They hung in his arms like a pair of rag dolls as he carried them toward the shack.

"What's up with this place?" Andy whispered.

"I don't know," Robin answered. But she had the horrible feeling that it had something to do with the story in the guidebook. If this was some kind of show, Robin didn't want to be a part of it. And if it wasn't a show, she and Andy were in serious trouble.

"Listen," she told her brother. "We've got to get out of here."

But it was too late.

The cart had jerked to a stop. Owen was already out of his seat and moving toward them.

Robin shrank back against Andy as the giant scarecrow stretched out his arms, ready to grab them.

CHAPTER 7

"Run!" Robin screamed as she pushed Andy off the back of the cart. "Run fast!"

But as Andy's feet hit the ground, Owen's gigantic fingers reached for the back of Andy's collar.

"Nooooooo!" Robin cried.

Andy spun around and kicked Owen in the knee. Owen moaned in pain, doubling over to grab his leg.

Robin leaped off the cart and tore past him. Together she and Andy made a mad dash for the fog.

"Hold on to my jacket, so we don't lose each other," Robin ordered her brother.

Andy grabbed the back of Robin's windbreaker as they disappeared into the mist.

"Mom! Dad!" Robin screamed. "Are you out here?" There was no reply.

"Mom! Dad!" she cried out again. "Where are you?"

"Stop screaming!" Andy said. "If Owen hears you, he'll find us!"

It was impossible to see anything in the fog. Robin couldn't even see her own hands as she waved them in front of her to keep from bumping into something.

Suddenly, the fog started to clear. In the distance, Robin could see the top of the giant shade tree in the middle of the parking lot.

"Andy, look!" Robin said, pointing ahead. "It's the parking lot! I bet Mom and Dad are waiting for us out there!"

Robin began to run faster, starting to feel relieved. Until she saw the parking lot. It was deserted.

"Hey!" Andy cried, noticing too. "Where are all the cars?"

Robin didn't care about *all* the cars. She cared about *their* car. *Why wasn't it in the parking lot, where they'd left it?*

"You don't think Mom and Dad left us here, do you?" Andy asked in a panic.

"Don't be stupid," Robin told him. "Mom and Dad wouldn't leave us."

"Then where are they?" Andy demanded. "And what happened to our car?"

Robin didn't have any answers. And she didn't have any time to think either. Dozens of ghouls with handcuffs and chains started filing out of the barn where the hayride had begun.

"It's time to chain up the children," the ghoul at the front of the line instructed the group. "Now move out!"

"Uh-oh," Andy gasped. "Something tells me we'd better get out of here before one of those ghouls sees us and chains *us* up!"

"We can't," Robin reminded him. "Not without Mom and Dad."

Just then the giant shade tree caught Robin's eye. "Do you think you can climb that tree?" she asked Andy.

"Sure," he answered. "Why?"

"If we can get to the top of it, we'll be able to see the whole orchard without anybody seeing us. Then maybe we can spot Mom and Dad," Robin said.

"Good idea," Andy agreed.

Robin and Andy dashed out from a row of hedges and ran straight for the tree. Robin hoisted Andy up to the lowest branch. Then she jumped up and grabbed it herself.

Within seconds, she and Andy were safely concealed among the tree's leafy branches.

Robin watched the ground for ghouls as she continued to climb her way to the top. As she reached for the next branch, she noticed something on the back of her left hand—an apple-shaped tattoo. In the center of it were the words "Zombie Number 459."

Robin's stomach did somersaults as her mind flashed back to the hayride, back to the moment when the branches had grabbed her arms and something cold and wet had pressed down on her hand.

34

"Andy!" Robin cried. "I think Yaga really is trying to turn the kids at the orchard into zombies!"

"You mean like the witch in Mom's guidebook?" Andy asked.

Robin nodded as she held up her hand for Andy to see.

Andy gasped. He had an apple stamp too. His read, "Zombie Number 458."

"I think the candy apples had something in them," Robin said.

"But we didn't eat any apples," Andy said. Then he quickly turned pale. "Uh-oh!" he gasped.

"What?" Robin demanded.

"Mom and Dad had apple cider!" he said. "Maybe *they* turned into zombies!"

Robin shook her head. So far she hadn't seen any grown-up looking zombies. Since the hayride, she had seen hardly any grown-ups at all, except for the ghouls. But they didn't count. "Mom and Dad are just missing," she insisted. "That's all."

Robin steadied her footing and peered out between the branches. From this high up, Robin could see the entire orchard spread out in front of her. The fog was completely gone.

She scanned every inch of the route they had taken on the hayride. There was no sign of her parents. The trail was deserted.

"Do you see them anywhere?" Andy asked.

"No," Robin answered.

"Me neither," Andy sighed.

Then something familiar caught Robin's eye.

"Andy!" Robin swallowed hard. "Look!"

She pointed to the far edge of the property, where dozens of ghouls were gathered around a lake. But the sight of the ghouls was nowhere near as terrifying as the sight of the cars . . . the cars that used to be in the parking lot!

Robin watched in horror as a gang of green ghouls pushed her parents' car into the lake.

CHAPTER 8

"*O*ooo-wen!"

The sound of Yaga's voice quickly pulled Robin's attention away from the lake and back toward the barn.

"*We're missing zombie children numbers 458 and 459!*" Yaga pushed her way past the ghouls with the chains. Peanut brittle slobber flew from her lips.

"Where are they?" Yaga bellowed. "Where are the last two zombie children? There are four hundred and fifty-nine children in Appleton, but only four hundred and fifty-seven of them are accounted for!"

Drusila scurried up beside Yaga. "I don't know *where* they are," Drusila said, "but I know *who* they are."

"Well, spit it out, you toothless little troll!" Yaga demanded.

"The two Carter urchins," Drusila said. "I found pictures of them in their father's wallet."

Robin felt like she was going to pass out.

Yaga stared at the pictures of Robin and Andy. "Where are their parents?" she asked.

"Safely secured with all the others," Drusila answered.

"And their car?" Yaga asked.

"At the bottom of the lake," Drusila said. "No one will ever know they were here."

"Good," Yaga said. "Now all we have to do is find their two mangy children."

Just then Owen stepped through the shrubs surrounding the parking lot.

He must have been following us, Robin thought. Owen was all out of breath.

"Where are the two Carter children?" Yaga bellowed.

Owen didn't answer. He just stood there, trembling.

"You let them get away, didn't you?" Yaga shrieked. "I should let the cat bite out your eyes for this!"

"Yeah, yeah." Drusila snickered devilishly. "Let the cat bite out his eyes this time. That's a good idea!"

Owen winced as he wiped Yaga's spit from his face. Robin almost felt sorry for him.

"If you don't find these two children and bring them back to me as zombies," Yaga threatened, "I *will* have your eyes bitten out. Only this time, I'll bite them out myself! Do you understand me?"

Owen nodded.

"Search the property!" Yaga commanded the others. "If I don't have all the children of Appleton by midnight tomorrow, I'll bite out *all* of your eyes!"

The ghouls took off in different directions to search for Robin and Andy.

"Come, Drusila," Yaga growled as she headed for the gift shop in the crooked old house. "We must secure the property."

Drusila shuffled away at Yaga's heels.

"Let's get out of here!" Andy whispered to Robin.

Robin shook her head. Then she put her finger to her lips and pointed downward.

Owen walked to the base of the tree.

As Robin and Andy looked down at him, he tilted his enormous head back and glared upward.

"Ooooooo-waaaaaay!" Owen moaned.

Robin's heart skipped six whole beats. She and Andy were doomed. Owen was going to reach right up and grab them!

But then, to her complete surprise, Owen didn't reach up. Instead he turned around and headed off toward the woods.

Robin sat stunned for a second.

"Whew," Andy said, echoing her relief. "I can't believe he missed us."

"I know," Robin agreed. "We got lucky that time, but we'd better get out of here before someone *does* see us."

"What about Mom and Dad?" Andy asked. "We can't just leave them here."

"If Yaga and her ghouls catch us, we're dead," Robin told him. "We've got to try to get away. Then we can tell somebody what's going on here."

Andy nodded. It was their only hope.

Robin scanned the ground below to make sure that the coast was still clear. In the distance, the light in the gift shop was on. Robin could see Yaga and Drusila through the front window. They were standing by the door, and Yaga was opening a big metal box on the wall. Inside the box were dozens of switches. Drusila studied them as Yaga filled her mouth with more peanut brittle from the giant jar that sat on the counter. The two of them looked too busy to notice Robin and Andy.

"Listen," Robin told her brother. "The second we hit the ground, run straight for the front gates, okay?"

Andy nodded. He was ready.

Robin dropped her leg down to the branch below and began to descend. But just as she reached the next branch, a loud, shrill sound wailed through the air and shook the tree.

Robin grabbed the branch above her and held on for dear life.

"Alarms!" Andy yelled. "They're sounding alarms!"

Dozens of floodlights snapped on all over the orchard. And from the top of the creepy old house a searchlight cut through the dusk and crisscrossed the grounds.

Within seconds, ferocious-looking dogs were let out of the barn by ferocious-looking ghouls.

"Listen up, you two Carter brats!"

Yaga's voice barked louder than the hounds ready to attack. It was booming through speakers on top of the gift shop.

"You're never going to get out of here alive!" Yaga's voice cackled. *"Never!"*

Giant sparks of electricity shot up from the iron fence that surrounded the property. They crackled like bolts of lightning.

Robin turned her head as a horrible screeching sound came from the big iron gates.

Her heart sank. Yaga was right. Their only hope of escape was sliding shut.

CHAPTER 9

Robin watched in horror as the front gates slammed closed with a shower of sparks.

"Oh, man," Andy sighed. "We're dead! There's no way we can get out of . . . "

Robin heard the *craaaaack* before Andy could finish.

"Oh, no!" Andy cried as the limb holding him snapped.

"Grab my hand!" Robin lunged to save her brother.

But it was too late. Andy was already falling, gathering speed as he plunged toward the ground.

Robin braced herself for the sickening thud of his body hitting the gravel below.

Andy flailed his arms, desperately trying to grab hold of the tree.

Suddenly, his shirt caught on a branch.

Robin let out her breath. "Are you okay?" she called down.

"I think so," Andy answered. He struggled to find footing. "I'm just scratched up, that's all."

Luckily, the wailing of sirens around the grounds had drowned out their screams. As Robin and Andy climbed down the tree, no one rushed over.

In fact, there didn't seem to be anyone around at all. Even Yaga and Drusila were gone. The lights in the gift shop were out.

Robin guessed that they'd headed to the orchards to join the search for her and Andy.

"We'd better get out of here now." Andy said exactly what Robin was thinking.

"I know," Robin answered. "But how?"

"Maybe we could climb over the fence," Andy suggested.

"No way!" Robin said. "Didn't you see all the sparks flying from that thing? It's electrified. If we try to climb over it, we'll be fried."

Suddenly Robin had an idea. "All we have to do is sneak into the gift shop and find the switch that opens the gate."

"Are you nuts?" Andy said. "What if we get caught?"

"We're not going to get caught," Robin insisted. "There's nobody around to catch us. Not now, anyway." Robin grabbed Andy by the arm and raced toward the gift shop.

"What if somebody's in there?" Andy said, trying to slow their pace.

"Nobody's in there," Robin replied. "The lights are out. It's dark inside."

It was getting pretty dark *outside* too.

Robin took a quick look behind her to make sure they were still alone as they reached the gift shop door. Then she pushed open the creaky door and slipped inside. Andy was right behind her.

"Ew, gross," Andy said, covering his nose. "It smells disgusting in here."

Andy was right. The air inside was thick and sour smelling.

"What kind of gift shop is this anyway?" Andy asked.

"Who cares?" Robin shot back. "It's not like we're planning to buy anything."

"Something tells me we wouldn't want to," Andy said.

It was too dark to see much of anything. But a quick glance around told Robin that the place was full of creepy-looking stuff that smelled putrid, like rotten eggs.

"You watch the outside," Robin told Andy as she stepped around the counter where Yaga's giant jar of peanut brittle stood. "Make sure no one comes this way."

Robin quickly located the metal box on the wall that Drusila had been studying.

"Oh, no," she groaned as she pulled open the box.

"What's wrong?" Andy asked.

"There are hundreds of switches in here," Robin answered. "None of them are marked. How am I supposed to know which one works the gate?"

"Just flip them all," Andy said. "Then we'll make a run for it."

Robin hesitated. It seemed dangerous—she had no

idea what any of the switches controlled. But what choice did she have? She hit the first switch. The lights in the gift shop came on.

Robin snapped them back off, hoping that no one outside had noticed.

She was terrified to touch the next switch. But she forced herself to do it. It was their only hope of escape.

That one set off alarm bells *inside* the gift shop.

Robin switched it off just as quickly as the first.

"Uh, Robin," Andy began. "We've got problems."

"No kidding," Robin shot back. "I'm never going to find the right switch."

"No," Andy said. This time he sounded frantic. "I mean, *big* problems!" He started backing away from door in terror. "Owen!"

Robin looked around desperately for a back door. But there was none. She and Andy were trapped.

CHAPTER 10

Owen's footsteps came closer.

"We've got to hide!" Robin whispered.

She looked around the dark room and spotted a stack of boxes in the corner.

"Over there!" She pushed Andy toward the boxes.

They scrambled behind them just as the door began to creak open.

The sound of heavy footsteps crossed the floor, heading in their direction.

Robin and Andy held on to each other, shrinking down as low as they could.

The footsteps kept coming.

Robin was dizzy with terror. Any second now, Owen would kick the boxes aside and grab them both.

The footsteps stopped. Owen stood on the other side

of the boxes. Robin could see the tips of his giant black shoes.

Robin put her hand over her mouth. She didn't even want to breathe. She didn't want to risk making any sound that Owen might hear.

All at once Owen's enormous hands reached out. But they weren't reaching for Robin or Andy. They were holding something. And he was reaching to put whatever it was high on the shelf against the back wall. Then he turned and headed back toward the door.

Robin waited to hear the door open. But that didn't happen. Instead she heard a drawer slide out. Then a loud click. And another. And another. Owen was flicking the switches.

Robin got up enough courage to peek around the side of the boxes. Owen was standing by the metal box, studying a paper he held in his hand. He flipped another switch. Then he put the paper back in the drawer under the counter and closed it.

Robin quickly ducked back behind the boxes before Owen looked in her direction. A few seconds later she heard the door creak shut.

Robin and Andy looked at each other.

"I think he's gone," Andy whispered.

Robin glanced around the room to be sure. Then she got up and headed toward the drawer in the counter.

"Robin?" Andy called after her.

"Shhh," she told him, pulling open the drawer. Inside was the paper Owen had been looking at.

"Oh, my gosh," Robin murmured.

The paper was a diagram of all the switches. Each one was clearly marked. Now all she had to do was find the switch that opened the gate.

"Robin!" Andy gasped.

She could tell by the tone of her brother's voice that something else was wrong.

Robin spun around to face the door, thinking that Owen had returned. But that wasn't it.

"Robin," Andy said again. "Look at this."

Andy stood in front of the shelves, pointing at something above him.

Robin moved toward him to look for herself. A small cry escaped her throat when she saw what it was.

Lined up in rows were hundreds of tiny figures that looked like shriveled-up people. They stood on the shelf, staring down at Robin and Andy with shriveled-up eyeballs!

CHAPTER 11

*T*hey're not real!

That was what Robin tried to tell herself. But they looked so lifelike.

"What *are* these things?" Andy asked, backing away from the shelves.

"They look like dolls," Robin answered. *"Creepy* dolls."

"Well, I hope they're creepy *dead* dolls," Andy shot back. "Because they look like miniature ghoul people."

Robin forced herself to reach up and touch one of the figures with the tip of her finger. She was half expecting it to move. But when it didn't, she lifted it off the shelf.

"You see," she told her brother. "They really are just dolls."

Robin examined the shrunken-headed figure in her hand as Andy reached up to grab one himself.

"Oh, man." He flinched the second he touched it. "These things are disgusting."

Robin had to agree.

The heads of the dolls were carved out of dried, shriveled-up apples. The faces were pockmarked and lumpy, where pieces of apple had been whittled away. Brown, rotting noses were chiseled between two apple-chunk cheeks, and two little nostrils were perfectly carved into tunnels.

Each doll had rigid red lips and eyeballs sunk deep into apple-hole sockets.

"Look," Andy said as he reached for another doll. "Every one of them is different."

Robin saw that he was right. No two dolls were alike. Each lumpy, gross face had its own disgusting features. Some of the dolls' noses were crooked. But others were chiseled straight down, like ski slopes, or pushed in like pug dogs', or puffed out like pigs'.

Even the hair on their heads was unique. There were different colors and styles and lengths, including a couple of dolls who were bald. Each one was dressed differently too. There were dolls wearing suits, dresses, jeans—even pajamas. There was even a shelf full of shriveled-up ladies in puffed-up mink coats.

But the creepiest thing about all the dolls was their shriveled-up eyes. Every eyeball seemed real—as if it was looking, and seeing! If the dolls didn't look so shriveled-up and dead, Robin would have thought there really was some kind of life behind their eyes.

Robin quickly put the doll in her hand back on the shelf. She couldn't stand to look at it one moment longer. Besides, they had more important things to worry about.

"Come on," she said to her brother. "Put that thing down. We have to get out of here."

But Andy was mesmerized by the doll he was holding. "Wait a minute," he said. "Who does this look like to you?" He held a plump doll in a suit up to Robin's face.

Robin pushed it away. "We don't have time for this," she told him.

"Just look at it, Robin," Andy insisted. "Please."

Finally Robin looked at the doll's face. Its chunky cheeks were puffed up like a chipmunk's. And its fat, lumpy nose stretched from one rotting ear to the other. Robin couldn't help thinking that the doll looked familiar, especially when she noticed a black mole on the top of its twisted lip.

She gasped. "It looks just like Mr. Hudson, the school principal!"

"Yeah," Andy agreed. "Pretty weird, huh?"

"*Really* weird," Robin said, shuddering as she gazed at the doll again. It looked *exactly* like Mr. Hudson.

"Look at this one," Andy told her, handing her another. "It looks like my teacher, Mrs. Cope." He pointed to the doll's head. "Her hair's even twisted into that beanie bun she always wears."

Andy was right. The doll did look exactly like Mrs. Cope.

"Maybe it's a coincidence," Robin said as she nervously studied the shrunken-headed teacher in her hand.

"Oh, yeah?" Andy shot back. "Well, here's one that looks just like Mr. Gentry."

"Who's Mr. Gentry?" Robin asked.

"The butcher Mom buys our meat from," he reminded her.

"Oh, right," Robin remembered.

"Look," Andy went on. "He's wearing that bloody apron he always wears. And he's even got a little meat cleaver in his hand."

Robin glanced at the rotting stump of a butcher. Then she started to scan the shelves again. "This is so strange," she said, growing more uneasy by the second.

There were dozens of figures Robin didn't recognize. But there were dozens she did. She picked out Mrs. Gibbs, the old lady who lived next door, dressed in the same dress she'd been wearing that morning when Robin saw her picking up her newspaper. She saw the video salesman from the video store, the gardener who took care of their lawn and raked the leaves, even the bus driver who drove them to school.

"There must be one of everybody in town," Robin said as she made her way along the shelves. "Why are they modeled after people who live in Appleton?"

"I don't know," Andy answered, picking up another pair. "Who are these two? I know I've seen them before."

Robin took a close look. She'd seen them before too, but she couldn't remember where. Until she noticed tufts of red hair shooting out of their rotting skulls.

The rooster-headed dolls in Andy's hands were the

parents of the redheaded kids on the hayride ahead of them! Their parents had been missing right after the hayride too! Just like Robin and Andy's!

Robin's head started to reel. As she looked up to the top shelf where Owen had just placed something, the feeling got much worse. Two more dried-up dolls sat there.

Nooooooooo! Robin's brain was screaming inside her head. *This can't be!* But as Robin stared at the doll on the left, there was no way to deny what was happening. She would recognize those emerald green eyes anywhere.

CHAPTER 12

An icy shiver went up Robin's spine as her eyes locked on the doll with the bright green eyes.

"Andy . . ." Robin managed to squeak, pointing to the top shelf.

Andy looked up. His face went pale. "It's Mom and Dad!" he gasped. "Isn't it?"

For a moment Robin couldn't speak. She'd never seen anything so horrifying. Her mother's beautiful face was squished-up and rotting. Her dad's funny grin was carved into a twisted sneer.

"Our parents are appleheads!" she shrieked. "Yaga and her ghouls turned Mom and Dad into appleheads!"

"Look how little they are." Andy gulped, staring up at their shrunken parents.

"We have to get them out of here," Robin said.

But neither one of them made a move to touch their parents.

Touching the appleheads was one thing when Robin thought they were dolls. But touching applehead *people* was a whole other story. Especially when they were her parents!

"Grab them," she finally ordered her brother.

"You grab them!" Andy shot back.

Robin's heart beat faster. There were footsteps passing by outside. They had to get out of there. Now!

Robin had no choice but to reach up for her parents.

Their bodies were squishy in some places, but brittle and hard in others. Robin was afraid she was going to break them in two as she lifted them from the shelf.

"Oh, man." She choked back a sob. "Poor Mom and Dad," she said. "Look at them, Andy. They're helpless."

Robin couldn't believe she was holding her parents in her hands. And she couldn't bear the sight of their eyes looking up at her, as if they were pleading for help.

Andy stared at them. "Mom," he said nervously. "Dad? Can you hear me?"

Robin expected the figures to squiggle or squirm. But they didn't move. They didn't answer.

The roving spotlights outside reminded Robin they had to go before Yaga found them.

"Here," she said, handing their parents to her brother. "Hold them while I find the switch that opens the gate."

"Aw, geez." Andy shuddered as he took the figures. "They feel so creepy."

Robin picked up the paper with the diagram and studied it. Finally she figured out which switch opened the gates.

"Go over to the door," she told Andy. "When the coast is clear, I'll flip the switch and we'll make run for it. Okay?"

"Okay," Andy agreed. "But you take Mom," he said, handing her over. "I can't run with both of them."

Robin took her mother. Then she watched nervously as Andy headed to the door, opened it just a crack, and peeked outside.

"All clear," he whispered over his shoulder.

"Okay," Robin said. "We'll go on the count of three. One. Two. Three!"

The instant Robin flipped the switch, Andy burst through the door. He was off and running, with Robin right behind him.

"Run, Andy! Run!" she screamed as she pushed herself to move faster.

They raced through the parking lot and headed down the gravel road. Robin could see the gates up ahead. They were beginning to open. But as they did, another siren began to blare.

Robin looked behind her, terrified that all the witches and ghouls would come after them now. The only one she saw was Yaga, running for the house. In seconds, the old witch would flip the switch and the gates would slam shut again.

"Robin!" Andy cried as he slipped through the iron bars. "Hurry!"

Robin reached the front gate just as Yaga hit the switch. Behind her, the gates came together with a clang.

"We did it!" Robin exclaimed, jumping up and down for joy. "We got away!"

"Careful!" Andy yelped. "You'll squish Mom!"

Robin was so excited to have escaped, she'd forgotten all about the applehead in her hand—the applehead that happened to be her mother.

Robin quickly lifted her mom to her face. "I'm sorry, Mom," she said. "I didn't mean to squeeze you so hard."

The applehead didn't reply.

"She doesn't hear you," Andy said sadly. Then he looked down at the applehead of a dad in his hands. "They probably don't even know that they're appleheads," he told Robin. "And they probably don't even know we're in trouble."

Andy was right. Their parents didn't hear them. And they didn't see them either. Worst of all, they couldn't help them. Robin and Andy were on their own.

Robin trembled as she peered through the darkness. Without her parents to protect her, she felt scared, even outside the orchard.

"I guess we should head home," Robin told her brother, looking up and down the dark, winding road.

"Which way is that?" Andy asked.

Robin thought about it for a second, trying to remember which way they'd turned when they drove into the orchard. "That way," she said, pointing to her left. "That's the way we came."

Robin and Andy started to walk. They were careful to stay far away from the fence that surrounded the orchard, so they wouldn't get electrocuted or grabbed.

Inside the orchard, the sirens still blared. As the searchlights crisscrossed the grounds inside the fence, they cast eerie shadows on the ground *outside,* shadows that looked like ghosts and ghouls. They made Robin and Andy jump.

"What's that?" Andy gasped, pointing to something ahead.

At first, Robin thought that Andy was just reacting to another shadowy figure. But she was wrong. The shadow Andy was pointing at was moving—right toward them!

CHAPTER 13

"Someone's coming!" Robin cried in a whisper.

"They know we escaped!" Andy cried back. "And now they're out *here* looking for us!"

Robin was about to grab her brother's hand and run in the opposite direction. But then they'd be running back to the gate, where more shadowy figures were surely waiting to grab them.

"Come on." Robin pulled Andy behind a tree on the side of the road. "Just keep quiet. Don't even breathe."

Robin watched as the shadow drew closer and started to take shape.

Is it Yaga and her ghouls? she thought. *Or Owen?*

A second later her question was answered.

The figures approaching weren't witches or ghouls. They were kids. Kids that Robin recognized!

"It's Christine and Katie and Jill! The girls that invited me to the Halloween party," Robin exclaimed. "What are they doing here?" Robin stepped out from behind the tree. "Christine!" she called out.

But Christine didn't answer.

"Hey, guys!" Robin rushed toward them. "Stop!"

None of them did. They just kept walking toward the front gate as if Robin didn't exist.

"Wait!" she cried, running after them. "Don't go in there. There's an evil witch and ghouls in that orchard. See—they turned my mom and dad into appleheads," she went on, holding up her mother. "And they tried to turn Andy and me into zombies!"

None of her friends reacted. They just kept moving toward the gate. Robin's heart stopped. Her friends were acting like *zombies!*

"Come on," Robin said, tugging Andy along. "Let's just get out of here!"

Robin and Andy ran. And ran. And ran. They didn't stop until they reached the end of the dark, winding road.

"We're almost there," Robin panted, clutching a cramp in her side. "Look," she told Andy. "We're on Main Street. Just a few more blocks and we'll be home."

Andy was gasping for air. "Can't we rest for a second?"

"No," Robin said, taking off again. "We've got to go home and call the police."

By the time Robin turned onto their street, the pain in her side had spread to every muscle in her body. But she wasn't about to slow down. Not when safety was just a few feet away.

But as Robin and Andy turned into the driveway of the familiar old house with the dark gray shutters, Robin's knees buckled beneath her.

Home wasn't a safe place to be after all.

CHAPTER 14

The house had been attacked.

Broken eggs and shaving cream were smeared all over the windows. Toilet paper was draped from tree to tree like giant spider webs. And the fifty-pound pumpkin that Robin and Andy had carved with their father was smashed into a thousand pieces in the driveway.

"Somebody trashed our house!" Andy cried. "Do you think it was the ghouls from the orchard?"

"No." Robin shook her head as she remembered what day it was. "Tomorrow's Halloween, so tonight's mischief night," she reminded her brother. "It was probably a bunch of stupid kids." At least she hoped that's all it was. "Let's get inside before somebody tries to attack *us*," she said, running for the front porch.

At the front door Robin let out a groan. "It's locked!"

She dug through her pockets, frantically looking for her keys. "Please tell me you have your house keys with you," she told Andy.

Andy shook his head.

"Terrific," Robin said. "Now we can't get in."

"Wait a minute," Andy said. "Dad always puts his keys in his pants pocket!"

"Look at how small Dad is!" Robin snapped at her brother. "Even if his keys *are* in his pocket, you know how small *they* have to be? There's no way they're going to open this door!"

"Maybe the back door's unlocked," Andy suggested.

They went around to the back of the house, but that one was sealed tightly too.

"Check the windows," Robin said.

Robin and Andy made their way around the house trying every window there was. None of them budged until they got to the one over the kitchen sink. That window slid right open.

Robin sent Andy in first.

Andy leaned through the window, put his parents down on the counter, then climbed in himself.

"Oh, no!" he wailed a second later. "Dad rolled off the counter onto the floor!"

"Is he hurt?" Robin asked, squeezing through the window after her brother.

"How should I know?" Andy replied. "He's an applehead!"

Andy picked up their father and brushed him off. "He looks okay," he announced. Then he picked up their mom and stood her up on the counter before she rolled to the floor too.

"We'd better put them somewhere safe before they get smushed," Robin said, climbing down from the counter herself.

"Like where?" Andy asked.

Robin noticed the fruit bowl on the kitchen table. "Put them in there," she told Andy, pointing to it.

"The fruit bowl?" Andy asked. "You want me to put Mom and Dad in a fruit bowl!"

"Where else should we put them?" Robin asked.

"I don't know," Andy shot back. "Maybe we should put them in the den so they can watch TV."

"Appleheads can't watch TV!" Robin said. "Put them in the bowl with the other fruit. At least they'll be safe there."

"I guess," Andy agreed finally. Carefully, he put their parents in the bowl, next to the bananas.

Robin picked up the cordless phone on the kitchen table and started to dial.

"What are you doing?" Andy asked.

"Calling the police," Robin said. "I'm going to tell them about the orchard."

The phone rang twice before a woman picked up and said, "Nine-one-one. What's the emergency?"

"I need the police," Robin said into the receiver.

"Hold on, I'll connect you," the voice responded. The phone clicked once before a different voice came over the line.

"Appleton police," a man's voice said. "This is Officer Walker."

"My name is Robin Carter," Robin blurted. "My brother and I need help right away."

"What seems to be the problem?" the officer asked calmly.

"This afternoon my parents took us out sightseeing around town," Robin started to ramble nervously. "And we ended up at the Appleton Orchard, which was supposed to be charcoal. At least according to my mother's guidebook," she went on. "It said that a bunch of angry parents burned it to the ground three hundred years ago after some evil witch turned all the kids into zombies with poisoned apples." Robin stopped to take a breath.

"I see," the officer said, sounding suspicious.

"Only it wasn't burned to the ground," Robin continued. "The orchard was open. And there really was an evil witch there. Her name is—"

The officer interrupted Robin. "Listen, kid." He sounded stern. "This line is for emergencies, not prank calls."

"This *is* an emergency!" Robin said. "The evil witch turned our parents into appleheads!"

"I thought you just told me that the evil witch turned all the kids into zombies," the officer shot back.

"She did!" Robin told him. "The adults are appleheads; the kids are zombies. I have a stamp on my hand to prove it!" she added.

The officer sighed loudly. "Where are your parents now?" he asked.

"Right here," Robin answered. "In the fruit bowl."

"Well, why don't you put one of them on the phone," he said.

"I can't!" Robin shouted into the receiver. "I told you, they're both appleheads!"

"I'm not so sure your mom and dad would be too happy to hear you call them that," the officer scolded. "Prank or no prank."

"This isn't a prank," Robin insisted. "There really is an evil witch! And my parents really *are* appleheads!"

"Yeah, yeah," the officer said. "And the last kid that called here tonight told me *his* parents were abducted by aliens. Now, I know that it's mischief night," he went on. "But the police department doesn't take kindly to practical jokes."

"This isn't a joke," Robin said.

"No, it's not," the officer agreed. "Tying up the police department's phone lines is not a joke. And if you call here again, I'm going to send some officers out there to talk to your parents."

"B-but . . . " Robin sputtered.

"But nothing," the officer cut in. "Have a happy Halloween." With a click the line went dead. Robin stood holding the phone in her hand.

"What did he say?" Andy asked.

"He didn't believe a word I told him," Robin said. "He thought I was making some kind of prank call."

"Maybe I should call him too," Andy said. "I bet he'll believe us if I say the same thing."

Robin doubted it, but she figured it was worth a shot. She was about to hand her brother the phone when, with a gasp, she dropped it. Someone was moving around outside the sliding glass doors in the kitchen!

The glass was covered with shaving cream, but Robin could definitely see someone. Someone big. Someone she had hoped never to see again!

Robin screamed as the horrible creature with the basketball-sized head pressed its painted-on face up against the glass. Owen, the scarecrow, was staring at her!

CHAPTER 15

"Owen!" Robin shrieked as she pointed to the sliding glass doors.

"Where?" Andy spun around to look. But Owen's face had disappeared.

"He was there a second ago!" Robin insisted. "I saw him!"

Someone pounded on the front door.

"Aaaaaaaagh!" Andy screamed. "He's trying to break in!"

Then the pounding stopped. That scared Robin even more.

"Uh-oh!" Robin gasped. "He's coming around to the kitchen again! Quick," she said, pulling her brother into the foyer. "We have to get upstairs."

Robin and Andy tore up the steps and into Robin's

room. They slid under the bed as fast as they could.

For a good ten minutes, they lay in the darkness, listening. But there was nothing to hear.

"You think he left?" Andy finally whispered.

"I hope so," Robin answered, starting to feel a little bit better. She crawled out from under the bed. Then she heard voices drifting up into her room from outside.

Andy heard them too. He gulped. "Who is that? Ghouls?"

"I don't know," Robin replied, terrified.

But the voices drifting through Robin's bedroom window weren't ghoul voices at all.

"It's kids!" Robin exclaimed a moment later. "Listen, Andy. They're just kids, laughing and shouting."

Andy was sitting on the bed biting his fingernails. "Are you sure?"

"Yes," Robin said, patting his shoulder. "They're probably doing Halloween mischief." Then she had an idea. "Maybe they can help us."

But as Robin crept over to the window, she started to have second thoughts. Maybe the kids who were laughing and shouting were kids from the orchard. Zombies who'd come with Owen!

A loud bang outside made Robin jump. Slowly she leaned over to peek out the window. Owen was nowhere in sight. But on the lawn was a group of kids running away from the house.

Robin wanted to open her window to call to them. But she was too afraid that Owen was hiding somewhere nearby.

Andy stood next to her. "Maybe we should call the police again," he suggested.

Robin shook her head. "They won't believe us." Then she remembered something Officer Walker had said. "Wait a minute!" she said. "You're right. We *should* call the police back again! That way they'll think it's another prank call. And then they really will send somebody out to talk to Mom and Dad!"

"Have you lost it, Robin?" Andy said. "The police can't talk to Mom and Dad. They're appleheads!"

"I know," Robin shot back. "But once the police get here, we can prove to them that we're not making up stories."

Robin reached for her phone and dialed. Once again she got connected to Officer Walker.

"Appleton police." His voice came over the line. "Officer Walker speaking."

"This is Robin Carter again," Robin said into the receiver. "My brother and I still need the police."

"Oh, really?" Officer Walker didn't sound amused. "What happened now?" he asked. "Did the evil witch turn *you* into an applehead? Or did she turn your brother into a zombie?"

"Neither," Robin told him. "But Owen, the evil scarecrow, is outside our house! And he's trying to break in!"

"Okay, kid," Officer Walker said. "I've had enough of this nonsense. What's your address? I'm coming out there myself to talk to your parents."

"Good," Robin said. "We're at twenty-four Applegate Drive," she told him. "Hurry!"

As the line went dead, Robin high-fived her brother. "They're coming!" she exclaimed triumphantly. "Now all we have to do is wait."

Robin and Andy waited nervously inside the house until they saw blue and red lights flashing through the darkness outside.

"They're here!" Robin cried.

She and Andy raced into the kitchen and scooped up their parents from the fruit bowl.

As Robin pulled open the front door, she saw the police car turn into the driveway. Then she saw something else.

"I don't believe it!" Robin said. "Those cops just ran over our mailbox!"

"Who cares." Andy pushed her out of the house. "At least they're here!"

Robin and Andy dashed across the lawn toward the car. It was sitting up on the curb, right where the mailbox used to be. Its blue and red lights were still flashing like crazy.

"Hey!" Andy said as they reached the car. "There aren't any cops in this car."

Robin didn't see anybody inside either.

But that's impossible, she thought.

"Hey, Officers." Robin tapped on the window.

No one responded.

"Where did they go?" Robin mumbled as she pressed her nose against the glass to get a better look.

But she wasn't prepared for what she saw.

CHAPTER

16

"The policemen are appleheads!" Robin yelled to Andy.

"What do you mean, the policemen are appleheads?" Andy asked.

"Look!" Robin pointed inside the car.

Two tiny applehead policemen sat on the front seat of the police car. They were dressed in uniform, complete with guns and badges.

Andy smashed his face against the window to see. "Oh, man," he cried a second later. "No wonder they crashed right into our mailbox! They can't even reach the steering wheel!"

"Wait a minute," Robin said, thinking out loud. "There's no way they could have been appleheads when they left the police station. Appleheads can't drive a police car. They're too short to even climb in."

"So they turned into appleheads *after* they started driving," Andy reasoned.

"Yeah," Robin said. "Right before they smashed into our mailbox."

"But what made them shrink?" Andy asked.

"I don't know," Robin answered. "But I'm going to find out."

Robin opened the door to the police car. Immediately she noticed the name on the badge the driver was wearing. Officer Walker.

"He's the one I talked to on the phone," she told Andy. "He definitely wasn't an applehead then."

Robin stuck her head in farther.

"What are you looking for?" Andy asked.

"A clue," Robin replied. "Maybe something in this car turned them into appleheads."

Robin saw exactly what it was. And she smelled it too.

"Look!" She pointed to two overturned coffee mugs. The contents had puddled on the floor of the car. "The policemen were drinking apple cider!"

"Do you think Yaga gave it to them?" Andy asked.

That's exactly what Robin was thinking. *Only how did Yaga do it?*

Suddenly she had a terrible thought. "What if Yaga and her ghouls have figured out a way to poison *all* the apples in Appleton?" she said.

"You mean like at school and in all the stores?" Andy asked.

Robin nodded.

Andy turned pale. "Then everybody who drinks apple cider or eats apples will turn into an applehead or a zombie!"

Robin nodded again, feeling as terrified as Andy looked.

"So how come there weren't any applehead *kids* at the orchard?" Andy asked.

"I don't know," Robin answered. "Maybe Yaga's poison works one way on adults, and another way on kids."

A strong burst of wind tore through the trees. A moan echoed through the air.

"Uh-oh." Andy was startled. "Is that Owen?"

Robin didn't know. What she did know was that she wanted to be back under her bed.

"Come on," she cried as she slammed the squad car door and took off across the lawn. "We'd better get back inside and lock all the doors!"

"What about the policemen?" Andy asked as he raced up behind her. "Should we put *them* in the fruit bowl too?"

"We'll get them tomorrow when it's light out," Robin said as she ran through the front door.

Once Robin and Andy were safely inside with the doors and windows bolted, Robin started to think again.

"What if Yaga really is the same witch that Mom was reading about in the guidebook?" she asked Andy as she paced the kitchen floor.

"What if?" Andy asked, confused.

"Well, then maybe we could find out more about her," Robin said.

"How?" Andy wanted to know.

"In the library," Robin replied. "They have all kinds of old newspapers and magazines in there. Maybe there's even a book about her."

"How's that going to help us?" Andy asked.

"Maybe if we find out about her, we can figure out a way to stop her," Robin suggested.

"Good idea," Andy agreed. "Is the library open now?"

"No," Robin said. "We'll have to wait until tomorrow. For now, I think we should try to get some sleep."

"Yeah, right," Andy said. "Like I'm really going to be able to close my eyes with Owen lurking around out there."

"Come on," Robin said, heading out of the kitchen. "We'll stay in my room. Under the bed."

Robin looked back at the fruit bowl before she switched off the kitchen light. "Good night, Mom. Good night, Dad. I love you."

"Me too," Andy added. Then they headed up to Robin's room and crawled under the bed.

It was going to be a very long night.

CHAPTER 17

Robin didn't sleep a wink. She just lay there, under her bed, listening to the wind howl and the windows rattle.

Finally it was daylight.

Even though Robin was exhausted, she and Andy had to get to the library as soon as it opened. She dragged herself up and headed downstairs.

Andy had already gone down to the kitchen, and when Robin arrived, he was eating a bowl of cereal. Sitting on the table facing him were their applehead parents.

"Happy Halloween," Robin grumbled.

It was supposed to have been a fun day. There was going to be a party at school, a big parade, and another party at Christine's house, too. But right now all Robin could think about was getting her parents back to normal.

"We're going to have to call school," Andy reminded her. "So they know we're not coming today. Just pretend that you're Mom and tell them we're sick."

"What a lousy reason to have a day off," Robin said as she picked up the phone. But she didn't dial. Not yet. She had to practice first.

"Hello, this is Mrs. Carter," Robin said, disguising her voice. "Robin and Andrew's mother." She looked over at Andy. "Do I sound like Mom?" she asked.

"You sound more like her than I would," he answered.

It was hardly the reassurance she wanted to hear. But it was going to have to do.

Robin started to dial. She was so nervous she could barely breathe. She'd never missed a single day of school before. And now she was calling up, pretending to be her mother.

Robin chewed on her thumbnail as she waited, hoping she wouldn't get caught. With each ring she got more and more nervous, knowing that at any moment someone was going to answer.

But after ten rings she started to wonder. *Why isn't anyone picking up?*

"Nobody's there," she told Andy as she paced the floor.

"Maybe they're all at the orchard," Andy said. "Don't you remember? We saw the principal there, and my teacher too. I bet you there are no adults at school today. They're probably all appleheads!"

Robin stared at him. What if Andy was right? "We've got to get to that library!" she said, hanging up the phone. "Now!"

Andy got up from the table. "What should we do with them?" he asked, pointing at their parents.

"Leave them here," Robin answered. "They'll be safer at home than with us."

Andy nodded, then he followed Robin outside.

The police car was still in front of the house with its lights flashing. When Robin looked in, she saw the two applehead policemen still sitting on the front seat.

The rest of neighborhood was deserted.

"Even Mr. Jones isn't out today," Andy said.

Robin looked across the street to where the old man lived. Mr. Jones was always out on the front porch in the morning, waving to everyone who passed. But today Mr. Jones was nowhere to be seen.

Without saying anything to Andy, Robin ran across the street and up the lawn to Mr. Jones's porch.

A little applehead doll sat on Mr. Jones's porch swing. Robin immediately recognized the old man's white hair and glasses. Beside him on the swing sat a cup of apple cider.

"Oh, no!" Andy cried as he came up beside Robin. "Not him too."

"We've got to find out what's going on," Robin said. "And how to stop it."

She turned and headed back down the street toward the library.

It was only eight blocks from their house to the library, but it felt like the longest walk of Robin's life.

The other streets were empty too. There wasn't a soul

to be seen. Robin was beginning to worry that she and Andy were the only two people in Appleton who weren't zombies or appleheads yet.

But just as they started up the walkway to the library, they saw someone else. It was a fireman hanging a banner about the Halloween parade over the library door.

"Maybe we can get him to help us," Andy said.

"No," Robin said. "He won't believe us any more than the police did."

The fireman didn't even notice them as they walked past him into the library.

Robin went straight to the librarian's desk. But there was no librarian, just an applehead sitting in the chair. A cup of cider was on the desk in front of her.

"How are we going to find a book now?" Andy asked. "There's nobody to help us."

"Follow me," Robin told him.

She knew exactly where to look for what they needed. The books about the history of Appleton were all the way at the back of the library. Robin knew that because she'd done a report about the founding fathers of the town. She only hoped there was some information in one of those books that could help them now.

"What are we looking for?" Andy asked as he followed Robin into the history aisle.

"I don't know," she answered. She didn't even try to keep her voice down. There was no point. They were the only ones in the library anyway.

"Try to find something about the orchard," Robin told Andy as she began scanning the shelves herself.

A title caught her eye right away. "Look at this," she said, nudging Andy. *"The History of Appleton Orchard."* It was a big, fat book. "There's got to be something in this book that will help us," she said, reaching for it.

She had to believe that was true. She was even beginning to feel a little hopeful—until she pulled the book off the shelf.

Through the space where the book had sat, Robin could see into the next aisle. Something moved, catching her eye.

Balanced on her tiptoes, Robin peeked through the space to see what it was.

But just as she did, a monster-sized hand shot out from between the books on the shelf and reached for her throat!

CHAPTER 18

The book in Robin's hands fell to the floor with a thud. Robin jumped back from the shelf, screaming in terror.

"It's Owen!" she cried. "We've got to get out of here!"

Robin pushed Andy down the narrow aisle, then tore off ahead of him. "Run!" she yelled at the top of her lungs.

Owen came after them. He headed toward the front doors of the library to block their escape.

"Oooog," he grunted at them.

Robin turned to her left and darted into the children's room. Andy was right behind her.

"How do we get out of here?" Andy cried.

Robin didn't answer. She just kept going. She ran through the first door she saw. She was already through it before she realized that the sign on the door said "Keep Out."

Robin tried to turn around, but Andy was right behind her, pushing her forward. She gasped as the two of them began to topple down a staircase. Robin was on the fourth step down when she finally managed to regain her balance.

Behind her Andy came to a stop too.

"Keep going!" he said.

The footsteps were coming closer and closer as Robin and Andy raced down the steps, taking them two at a time. The steps led down to the basement. It was a dark, dingy place. The air was so musty, Robin began to sneeze. The sneezes sounded like explosions as they bounced off the cinder block walls and echoed all around them.

"Shhh," Andy said, slapping his hand over Robin's mouth. "With all the noise you're making, he'll find us for sure."

The door at the top of the stairs opened slowly.

Robin looked around, frantically trying to find some way to escape from Owen. But there was no way out of that basement besides the stairs. The few grimy windows in the room were up high, and they were far too small for a person to squeeze through. There was no question about it. They were trapped.

CHAPTER 19

"Over here," Andy whispered suddenly. He motioned toward a huge file cabinet in the corner.

The two of them ducked behind the file cabinet as Owen flicked on the light.

Robin held her breath, too scared to move. The room was silent.

What is Owen doing? she wondered.

As if to answer, a loud crash echoed right over her head. It sounded as though Owen had jumped up on top of the file cabinet.

Robin and Andy both screamed as they held on to one another for dear life.

It's over, Robin thought. *Owen's got us now.*

Robin was hoarse by the time she realized no one had grabbed them. Her scream trailed off as she looked up at the top of the file cabinet. Owen wasn't there.

Surely he knew where they were.

So where was he? And what was he doing?

Robin put her hand over Andy's mouth to quiet him. When he was silent, she put her finger to her lips to signal him to stay quiet. He nodded. Then, slowly and cautiously, Robin raised herself up until she could just barely see over the top of the file cabinet.

There was no sign of Owen.

Robin stood a little higher.

He was gone. She was sure of it.

She was about to heave a sigh of relief. Then she saw what had crashed on top of the file cabinet.

It wasn't Owen. But it was a present from him.

CHAPTER 20

"What is that?" Andy demanded. He stood up and came over to Robin. Together they stared at the thing Owen had left.

Slowly Robin reached out and picked up the small leatherbound book from the top of the file cabinet.

"It looks like it's a million years old," Andy said.

Robin nodded. The book's leather was cracked, and the edges of the pages were crumbling. Robin was afraid that if she tried to open it, the whole thing would fall apart.

She looked on the cover and spine for a title. But there wasn't one. Then, very carefully, Robin opened the book to the first page.

It was a diary.

"This *is* really old," Robin said, reading the date on the first page. "'October 31, 1896.'"

"Wow! This was written a hundred years ago," Andy said. "Whose is it?"

Robin began reading aloud.

"'My name is Martha Grant. I am twelve years old. I hope that someday, a hundred years from now, somebody reads this diary.'"

"A hundred years from now!" Andy echoed, checking the diary's date again. "That's exactly today!"

Robin nodded. "This is too weird," she said. Then she went on reading.

"'Something terrible has happened in Appleton. A horrible witch named Yaga appeared at the orchard the day before Halloween. She poisoned all the town's apples. And she used them to turn the adults into shriveled-up applehead dolls and the children into zombies.'"

"We were right!" Andy declared. "Yaga's poison works differently on grown-ups than it does on kids!"

"If only Mom and Dad hadn't . . ." Robin's voice trailed off. A lump rose in her throat.

"So what happened to everybody?" Andy asked, sounding afraid to hear the answer.

Robin forced herself to read on.

"'Tonight, at the stroke of midnight, the orchard began to burn. Yaga burst into flames and disappeared. At first I was relieved. But as soon as Yaga was gone, everyone else within the gates of the orchard disappeared too. Even the zombie children and the applehead adults. My own brother and parents have disappeared. Appleton is completely deserted. I am all alone.'"

Robin stopped reading, and she and Andy just looked at one another. Robin could tell that Andy was thinking the same thing she was. If they didn't do something to save their parents and their friends, they would end up just like Martha Grant—alone in a ghost town.

CHAPTER

21

"Why is Yaga doing this?" Andy asked.

Robin scanned the pages of Martha Grant's diary, looking for the answer. It didn't take her long to find it.

"'In 1696,'" Robin read on, "'several children from Appleton died after eating apples from Yaga's orchard. Angry parents stormed the grounds and set fire to Yaga's orchard. Yaga walked into the flames before the angry parents could bring her to trial. Before she disappeared in the flames, she put a curse on the town. She vowed that she would return to Appleton every hundred years to wreak her revenge.'"

"We've got to stop her," Andy declared.

Robin agreed. *But how?* she wondered. She kept reading silently, hoping to find the answer in the pages of Martha Grant's diary.

"We need help," Andy went on. "I think we should go to the police station. We can show them the diary. Then maybe they'll believe us."

"Not yet," Robin said, without taking her eyes off the page. "I don't want to hand this diary over to anyone until I've read every word."

Robin was sure that there was important information in the diary. Maybe even a way to get rid of Yaga once and for all. Why else would Martha Grant have written it?

Robin was right. Martha Grant did have a plan to get rid of Yaga. There were only two problems with it. Since no one had ever tried it before, it might not work. And it was very, very dangerous. But it was their only hope.

"Come on," Robin said to Andy as she closed the diary and headed for the stairs. "We don't have much time. And there's a lot we have to do."

"Why do you think Owen gave us this diary?" Andy asked as they went up the stairs.

"I've been wondering that too," Robin said.

"Maybe he's trying to help us," Andy suggested.

Robin shook her head. "If Owen's trying to help us, then why did he let Mom and Dad drink the poisoned apple cider in the first place? And why did he grab at my throat before?"

Andy shrugged. "I don't know," he admitted.

Owen was up to no good; Robin was sure of it. "He probably just wants to scare us even worse than we already are," she told Andy.

"Well, he's doing a really good job of it," Andy replied.

At the top of the stairs, Robin pushed the door open a crack and peeked into the library. No one was there.

She stuck her head out and looked around. Still no one.

"Let's go," she said to Andy.

They moved quickly, keeping careful watch around them. They made it through the children's room, through the lobby, and out the front door.

The cool, fresh air felt good, especially after the dark, musty basement. Robin sucked in a deep breath and felt herself start to relax a little. Now that they had a plan, at least there was hope.

But then she saw something in front of her. Something as horrifying as anything she'd seen so far.

CHAPTER

22

"Ewwwwwwww, gross!" Andy cried at the horrible sight.

The fireman who had been hanging the banner outside the library had fallen off his ladder. But that wasn't the worst of it. Now he was an applehead. And a squirrel was nibbling away at him!

"Shoo!" Robin hollered at the squirrel, stomping her foot on the pavement to scare it away.

It didn't work. The squirrel looked up at her for a second. Then it went right back to munching on the fireman's head.

"Oh, man." Andy cringed. "We can't let that squirrel eat his brains out!"

"Throw something at him," Robin suggested in a panic.

Andy bent down to snatch up a pebble from the ground. Then he tossed it at the squirrel, hitting the animal in the hind leg.

The startled squirrel jumped two feet in the air, let out an angry squeak, then took off like a shot.

Andy headed toward the applehead fireman.

Robin hung back. She didn't want to see what the squirrel had done to him. She was afraid that the squirrel had nipped off his nose or nibbled out his eyes.

"It's not so bad," Andy told her as he picked up the fireman. "The squirrel just took a little chunk out of the back of his head." Andy held out the applehead for Robin to see.

But Robin didn't want to see. "Cover it up with his hair," she told Andy.

Andy did that. Then he started to place the fireman back on his ladder.

"No." Robin stopped him. "Bring him with us. We'll show him to the police. With him and the diary, they'll have to believe us."

"Good thinking," Andy agreed. "Let's go."

The police station was right across the street from the library.

The two of them dashed down the walkway in front of the library and paused to look both ways before crossing the street.

No cars, Robin thought. That was odd. There was always plenty of traffic in town. But not today. *Why?*

Robin didn't have much time to think about it.

A moment later she and Andy burst through the front doors of the police station like a S.W.A.T. team.

The place was empty.

"Hello," Robin called out.

The only answer she got was the eerie echo of her own voice.

"Is anybody here?" she called louder as she and Andy moved into the front office.

"Look," Andy said, pointing to the chair behind one of the desks.

Before she even looked over the top of the desk, Robin knew what she was going to see. An applehead policeman.

Every chair at every desk in the front office was occupied by an applehead. And sitting on every desk was a cup of cider.

"Isn't there anybody in this town who *didn't* drink apple cider?" Robin groaned. "Come on," she said, moving down the corridor. "Let's check out the rest of the station."

Andy followed.

They went into every room until they reached the last office in the building.

"She did it," Andy said as he laid the applehead fireman on the applehead police chief's desk. "Yaga's already poisoned the whole town."

"No." Robin refused to believe it. "There's got to be someone left."

As if to prove her point, a door creaked open. There was the sound of footsteps.

"See?" she told Andy. She was about to call out, but something stopped her.

It was the footsteps. They didn't sound right.

Robin quickly put a finger to her lips to signal Andy to stay quiet. Then she listened.

The footsteps were coming closer. And there were lots of them. But it didn't sound like people walking normally.

Robin looked around the office for someplace to hide. She found a closet, and she and Andy managed to duck into it in the nick of time.

Robin was pulling the closet door shut when the shuffling feet came into the office.

As Robin caught a peek of who the feet belonged to, she was glad that she and Andy had stayed quiet. It wasn't help that had arrived. It was zombies!

CHAPTER 23

Robin and Andy stayed hidden inside the closet until they no longer heard any movement in the room.

"I think they're gone," Robin whispered.

She pushed open the door and peered out. The room was empty. Nervously she crept out of the closet.

"What were they doing here?" Andy whispered, coming out behind her.

Robin wasn't sure. But she had a hunch.

"Look," she said, pointing to the desk. "The fireman's gone. So is the police chief. The zombies must have taken them."

"Why?" Andy asked.

Robin shrugged. She didn't know, but it didn't matter right now. All that mattered was finding another real person in Appleton.

"Let's go to the fire station," Robin suggested. "Maybe there's someone there."

Andy nodded.

They headed back through the building toward the exit. Every office *really* was empty now. All the zombies were gone. So were all the appleheads.

When they opened the door to go outside, Robin and Andy stopped dead in their tracks. The town was full of zombie children! They shuffled along, up and down the streets, going from building to building. In their arms were dozens of appleheads.

"Oh, my gosh," Andy breathed. "Do you think Yaga sent all these zombies out to get all the appleheads?"

Robin nodded. "We've got to get home," she said in a panic. "Before the zombies get Mom and Dad too."

"Unless they've already got them!" Andy added.

Robin and Andy took off down the street.

Surprisingly, the zombies didn't pay any attention to them. They were too busy collecting appleheads.

The farther away from the center of town they got, the fewer zombies they saw.

"Maybe they haven't gotten to our neighborhood yet," Robin said hopefully. Or maybe they'd already been there.

Robin and Andy turned onto Applegate Drive.

The muscles in Robin's legs were burning, but the instant she saw her house, she pushed herself to run even faster. Andy stayed right beside her.

There wasn't a zombie in sight as they dashed up the

porch steps. Robin fumbled nervously with the key. Finally she managed to get the front door open.

"Mom!" she called out. "Dad!"

Of course there was no answer. Robin didn't really expect one.

She ran for the kitchen with Andy right behind her. She stopped short in the doorway, her eyes fixed on the kitchen table.

Andy crashed into her.

"Are they . . . " Andy didn't finish the question.

"They're still here!" Robin exclaimed.

Robin was relieved her parents were okay. But she knew her problems were far from over.

They still had to face Yaga. And they had to do it alone.

Robin sat down at the kitchen table and started to read Martha Grant's diary again before they headed back to the orchard, to be sure that she hadn't missed a thing.

There was only one way that Robin and Andy might save Appleton and their parents. Robin stared at the words on the page: *To defeat Yaga you must turn her own magic against her. Give her a taste of her own poison.*

But how?

CHAPTER 24

"Hurry," Robin said as she and Andy pedaled their way through the darkness.

It had been well past nine o'clock when Robin and Andy got on their bikes and headed for the orchard. Robin was terrified that they would never make it in time. According to Martha Grant's diary, they had to defeat Yaga before midnight, and midnight was less than three hours away. And they still had to figure out a way to sneak into the orchard without being seen.

Robin and Andy were dressed all in black. Both wore baggy pants with deep pockets. In the left pocket, each of them carried one of their parents. In the right pocket, they each held a weapon—a spray bottle of poison cider, which they'd collected from mugs left around town. It was what they'd use to try to defeat Yaga.

"Are you sure your plan is going to work?" Andy asked as he struggled to keep up.

"Of course it's going to work," Robin said. She hoped she sounded braver than she felt.

The two of them rode on in silence. A few minutes later, the iron bars surrounding the orchard came into view.

Robin and Andy slammed on their brakes.

Robin couldn't believe it. She'd spent all night trying to figure out how to get past the gates, and now they were wide open!

But, as it turned out, that wasn't very good news. A bunch of ghouls was standing near the entrance, observing the long line of zombie kids that was filing through.

"Oh, no," Robin mumbled. "What are we going to do? There's no way we can get past those ghouls . . . " As she stared at the line, she suddenly had an idea. "Hey, Andy. Do you think you can pretend to be a zombie kid?"

"No way, Robin," he said, shaking his head. "We're not getting in that line!"

"We have to," Robin insisted. "It's the only way we'll get inside. Don't you want to help Mom and Dad?" she pleaded.

Andy couldn't say no to that.

Robin's legs shook as she climbed off her bike and ditched it on the side of the road. She and Andy were about to enter the orchard. But would they ever make it out again?

Robin waited for Andy to get off his bike, then she started moving toward the line of zombies.

"Wait." Andy stopped her.

"What now?" she asked impatiently. They didn't have any time to waste.

"Look at those zombie kids," he said. "They're all carrying appleheads."

Andy was right. Every single zombie kid had at least one applehead in his or her hands. If Robin and Andy weren't carrying appleheads too, somebody would notice.

She reached into her pocket and produced her own applehead. "I'll carry Mom," she told Andy. "And you carry Dad. That way we'll blend right in."

Slowly Andy reached into his own pocket and pulled out his father. "I'm not going to let anything bad happen to you," he said to the applehead. "I promise."

Robin hoped it was a promise they could keep.

"Now just follow my lead and act like a zombie," she told him.

Robin and Andy shuffled over to the back of the line, trying to walk like the rest of the kids.

"This isn't going to work," Andy whispered in a panic.

"Shut up," Robin whispered back. "Zombie kids don't talk!"

"And they don't shake like you're shaking either," Andy shot back.

Robin *was* shaking. Especially when she saw what was going on at the front of the line.

"Andy." It was Robin's turn to panic. "Do you still have your zombie stamp?"

Andy looked at his hand. "Yeah," he answered. "Why?"

"Because the ghouls are checking everybody's hands for the stamp," she said.

"Uh-oh," Andy whispered. "What if those ghouls remember our numbers? What if they realize we're the kids who were missing?"

"No way," Robin said. "Those stupid ghouls will never remember the numbers on our hands."

Only the ghoul that was waiting to check Robin's and Andy's hands wasn't a ghoul at all. It was a scarecrow. And Robin was sure that *this* scarecrow would definitely remember their faces.

CHAPTER 25

Owen looked Robin right in the eye.

She could feel her whole body tremble as she waited for him to grab her and turn her over to Yaga.

But Owen didn't even look at Robin's stamp as she held up her hand. He just stared hard into her eyes.

Robin had to force herself to keep moving. She could feel Andy plodding along behind her. Owen had let them pass. *Why?*

Although Robin desperately wanted to turn around to see if Owen was following them, she didn't dare. The ghouls would notice for sure.

But she couldn't dwell on Owen, either. There were bigger problems up ahead.

Drusila, the witch, stood behind a huge basket. As the zombie children passed her, they were dropping their applehead people into her basket.

Robin held on to her mother so tightly, she was afraid she might crush her.

No way, Robin thought. *I can't drop Mom into that basket!* Who knew what would happen to her parents once they got into Drusila's clutches?

Robin tried frantically to think of something to do. She was only two zombies away from Drusila's basket.

The zombie in front of Robin dropped her appleheads into the basket and moved on.

Now it was Robin's turn. She reached out over the basket, but her fingers froze, refusing to let go of the applehead.

Drusila whacked Robin's knuckles with a stick. Hard.

Robin didn't dare cry out. Instead she opened her hand. Her mother tumbled into the basket with a sickening *thud.*

CHAPTER

26

Robin choked back a sob as she moved ahead with the rest of the zombies. Behind her, Andy dropped their dad into the basket too.

Robin forced herself to stop thinking about her parents. She couldn't cry—it was too dangerous. She had to figure out what to do next to put her plan into action.

Up ahead, the leader of the line of zombies was heading straight for the barn. Robin could see ghouls waiting there to secure them all with handcuffs and chains. She and Andy had to break free, now!

"Andy," Robin suddenly whispered over her shoulder. "When I say 'go,' run for the bushes."

Robin looked around slowly. It was very dark, and the ghouls were all busy. If she and Andy ran fast enough, maybe no one would notice.

"Go!" she cried, the second she thought the coast was clear.

Andy darted through the bushes like a jackrabbit with his tail on fire.

Robin was right behind him. Together they crouched down in the shrubs.

"I can't believe it!" Andy exclaimed in a whisper. "We made it. No one saw a thing!"

"We have to get to that gift shop," Robin told him.

"There are too many ghouls around," Andy said.

"We'll just have to wait until they chain up all the zombie kids," Robin told her brother. "Maybe then they'll go away."

But that didn't happen. Just moments later, Yaga tore through the parking lot. *"Where are those two zombie children?"* she screeched at Owen.

Owen put his head down.

"You didn't find them, did you?" Yaga wailed. She shook the scarecrow hard.

Owen moaned, sounding as terrified as Robin felt.

"There's only one hour left!" Yaga screamed. "If I don't have zombie children numbers 458 and 459, my plans will be ruined!"

Drusila scurried over. "There are no children left in town," she informed Yaga. "Every house in Appleton has been searched, and every applehead is accounted for."

"Then those two Carter brats must be *here* somewhere," Yaga bellowed. "Find them!"

Yaga stormed over to the ghouls by the barn.

"Unchain these zombies!" she ordered. "I want every breathing body searching for those two little urchins! And sound the alarms!" she added.

"Uh-oh," Andy gasped as the searchlights snapped on and alarm bells started to ring. "Here we go again!"

"Time is running out!" Yaga shouted.

Robin's stomach churned. That was exactly what she was thinking.

CHAPTER

27

As the ghouls and zombies set out to search the property, Robin and Andy plodded zombielike to the gift shop. Time really was running out. They had to move fast.

The door was unlocked, and the shop was empty. Robin was amazed at how easy it was for her and Andy to get inside. It was so easy that for a minute she was afraid it might be some kind of trap.

"Watch outside," Robin told Andy. "Make sure nobody is coming."

Andy kept the door open a tiny crack so that he could peek through it.

Robin headed over to the counter, to where Yaga kept her jar of peanut brittle. She took the lid off the jar, then pulled the squirt bottle of apple cider out of her pocket.

"Here goes," she mumbled.

Carefully, she sprayed the peanut brittle with the cider. She wanted to make sure that she got every piece. But she also had to be careful not to get it too wet. If it was too sticky and gooey, Yaga would know that there was something wrong with it and then she might not eat it.

Give her a taste of her own poison. Martha's words were burned into Robin's brain. *It's the only way to break Yaga's evil spell.*

"I hope this works," Robin said when she was through. She placed the lid back on the jar. "Now let's get out of here," she said to Andy.

"We can't," Andy replied. "Yaga is coming, with a bunch of witches and ghouls."

"What?" Robin started freaking out. But then she realized that the sooner Yaga came into the gift shop, the sooner she would probably eat a piece of peanut brittle. And that was exactly what Robin wanted.

Robin didn't have to tell Andy to hide. He darted behind the boxes in the corner even before she did. Robin barely made it before the door creaked open.

"Somebody had better find those two little brats," Yaga bellowed, "or I promise, you will all pay dearly!"

Yaga was so busy having a fit, Robin was afraid she wouldn't think about eating the peanut brittle.

"Someone will find them," Drusila croaked.

Then Robin heard someone take the lid off the jar of peanut brittle. She knew it was Yaga.

Robin almost giggled. *In just a few short minutes this*

whole nightmare will be over, she told herself. And she and Andy would be right there watching when Yaga ate her own poison and turned into an applehead. It was actually a stroke of good luck that she and Andy were trapped inside the gift shop.

Or so Robin thought.

Suddenly the boxes in front of them crashed to the ground. It was Drusila who'd kicked them aside. "There they are," the old hag snarled.

Robin was too startled to scream. She just stared at Yaga, who had been about to bite into a piece of peanut brittle. If one more second had passed before they'd been caught, everything would have been all right, but now it was over.

Robin watched in horror as Yaga threw her peanut brittle onto the floor. "Now you will pay for all the trouble you caused me," the old witch cackled.

CHAPTER 28

Drusila grabbed Robin and held her tightly. One of the other witches grabbed Andy.

"Bring them outside," Yaga screamed. Then she stormed out the door.

Robin kicked and screamed as Drusila wrestled her out the door behind Yaga. The other witch dragged Andy outside. He was putting up an even bigger fight than Robin. But it was useless.

We blew it, Robin thought. *We didn't save Mom and Dad or anyone else in Appleton. And now we can't save ourselves.*

According to Martha Grant's diary, everyone in the orchard would disappear at midnight in a burst of fire.

Outside, the sky was pitch black. Robin didn't have to look at her watch to know midnight was just moments away.

"Bring me two apples," Yaga ordered Owen. "Fast!"

Owen scrambled to obey. Quickly he produced two chunks of apple. Robin shuddered as she saw the worms dangling from them.

Yaga snatched up the apples and stomped over to Andy.

A bunch of ghouls had wrestled Andy to the ground. They held him down so that Yaga could drop the apple chunk into his mouth.

"There's no use trying to fight me," Yaga sneered as she knelt down beside him.

Andy moved his head from side to side to avoid the apple chunk that Yaga pressed against his closed lips. The ghouls held him steady. Yaga held his nose. Still Andy refused to open his mouth.

He held his breath for a long time. But it wasn't long enough. The instant he parted his lips, gasping for air, Yaga dropped the apple in.

"Hold his mouth shut," she told the ghouls. "Make sure he swallows."

Robin's heart pounded as Yaga turned toward her.

"You hold her for me," she ordered Owen.

Drusila handed Robin over to Owen.

Yaga cackled as she headed toward Robin holding out the chunk of wormy apple. Robin sealed her lips tightly. Nothing would make her open her mouth.

"Hold her nose," Yaga told Owen.

Robin took one last, deep breath.

But Owen didn't grab her nose. Instead he pushed her aside so hard that she fell to the ground.

"Owen!" Yaga screeched. *"Noooooooooo!"*

For a second, Robin didn't understand what was going on. Then she looked at Owen. The scarecrow had grabbed Yaga and was holding her tight.

"I-er," Owen bellowed at Robin. "I-er!"

"What?" Robin cried.

Small flames appeared at the hem of Yaga's skirt. It was midnight. Yaga was starting to burn! In a few more minutes, everyone else would burn too.

Drusila and the other witches charged at Owen, trying to force him to let go of Yaga. But Owen was bigger and stronger. He managed to keep them at bay and hold on to Yaga at the same time. But there was no telling how long he could keep it up.

"I-er!" Owen yelled impatiently at Robin.

Robin thought he was saying "fire." But then Owen hollered again. "Sssss-i-er!"

Suddenly Robin understood what Owen wanted. Cider!

She scrambled to her feet and pulled the bottle of cider out of her pocket. It was still half full.

The flames were licking their way up Yaga's skirt. "I—er!" Owen demanded again. He was having a hard time holding on to the burning witch. But he wasn't giving up.

Robin popped the lid on the bottle as Yaga let out a blood-curdling scream. Then Robin turned the bottle toward Yaga and squeezed hard, sending a stream of Yaga's own cider into the evil hag's mouth.

That's it! Robin thought triumphantly. *I got her. Now the curse is broken!*

But instead of stopping the fire, Robin's spray of cider only seemed to ignite the blaze. The flames at Yaga's feet exploded, as if they'd been doused with lighter fluid.

Then, in a wild burst of sizzling fire, Yaga disappeared.

CHAPTER 29

"N$_{ooooooooo}$!" Robin cried. "I was too late!" Frantically, she gazed all around, waiting to see the flames engulf everyone else in the orchard.

Andy had spit out the wormy apple and was screaming too. But it took Robin a full minute to realize what her brother was saying.

"Look! It worked!" he yelled, pointing at Owen's shoes. "Look at Yaga!"

As the smoke started to clear, Robin saw that Yaga had not disappeared at all. She was still there, standing between Owen's enormous black shoes. Only now Yaga was six inches tall, and the ugliest-looking applehead Robin had ever seen.

"We did it!" Robin rejoiced. "We really did it!"

She was so happy, she didn't notice Drusila and the gang of ghouls surround her.

"You killed her!" Drusila wailed. "Now *you* must be killed!" Drusila lunged for Robin's throat. But as she reached out, she herself vanished into thin air.

So did all the rest of the ghouls.

All but Owen, who started to cry.

"You saved my life," he said. "If you two hadn't come along, I—"

"You can talk!" Andy cried, staring at the scarecrow in amazement.

Robin was stunned. Owen *was* speaking—and his voice was gentle and his words were clear.

"Now that Yaga's curse is broken, I can speak," Owen explained. "The moment the evil old hag disappeared, I got back my tongue. Thank you," he added, "for saving my life."

Robin smiled. "No," she told Owen. "You saved *our* lives."

"Why did you help us?" Andy asked.

"Because Yaga is a horrible creature," Owen replied. "And because I didn't want you to be left all alone like my sister," he added sadly.

"Your sister?" Robin repeated. "Who's that?" But suddenly she knew. It was the girl in the diary. *That* was why Owen had left the diary for them.

"My sister was named Martha," Owen explained. "When we were little, our parents brought us here for a hayride too. And Yaga gave us apples and cider to take on the ride. Just like she gave them to you. Only Martha didn't like apples," Owen went on. "So I ate them both."

Robin thought about her own parents and started to cry too. "So Yaga turned you into a zombie, and your mom and dad into appleheads," she said sadly.

"Worse," Owen went on. "Yaga was so mad that Martha got away, she decided to take it out on me. She didn't want to leave me a zombie like the rest of the kids, because then I wouldn't remember a thing. So she took out my tongue and gave back my memory. That way, I'd remember every evil thing she had done to my parents and Martha and the rest of the town, but I wouldn't be able to tell a soul. For the past hundred years, I've been Yaga's personal slave."

"So you're like a hundred years old then, huh?" Andy asked Owen.

"A hundred and ten," Owen answered. "But my heart's still young." He took off his scarecrow mask. His face was more wrinkled than any face Robin had ever seen. But it wasn't scary looking at all. It was gentle and kind. His black, giant eyes shone with joy.

"Wait a minute." Robin suddenly had a thought. "How come you didn't disappear with all the witches and ghouls?" she asked Owen.

"Because I helped break the curse," he explained. "I've been reading about breaking curses in Yaga's books. That's how I knew what to do."

"What about our mom and dad?" Andy asked. "And everybody else in Appleton?"

Robin had been wondering the same thing.

"It's too late for the kids from hundreds of years ago," Owen answered. "But you've saved everybody who was at the orchard yesterday."

"So where are they?" Robin looked around.

"Just be patient," Owen said. "This curse-breaking takes a few minutes."

Robin looked at Owen, confused.

"Don't worry," he told her. "Everything is going to go back to the way it was before Yaga reappeared. It'll be as if none of this ever happened."

"You mean our parents won't even know they were appleheads?" Andy asked.

"Right," Owen said. "In just a few seconds, it's going to be yesterday again."

"Get out of here." Robin couldn't believe it.

Owen grinned. "Watch," he told them. "Even the sun is going to come back out."

"Yeah, right." Andy couldn't believe it either.

But Owen was telling the truth. Seconds later, it started to happen. The sun was rising. But it wasn't rising in the east. It was rising in the west. And it was crossing the sky backwards.

The cars that the ghouls had pushed into the lake were rolling out of the water and back to the parking lot—in reverse.

Even the hands on Robin's watch started spinning backward.

"This is too cool!" Andy exclaimed, watching in amazement.

Robin thought it was pretty cool too. Especially when the coolest thing of all happened.

"Look!" Robin shrieked, pointing toward the gift shop. "Here come Mom and Dad!"

They were walking out of the gift shop holding hands, acting just as goofy as ever.

CHAPTER 30

"Mom! Dad!" Robin and Andy exclaimed as they ran for their parents. "You're not appleheads anymore!"

"Excuse me?" Mrs. Carter said.

"You're not an applehead!" Robin repeated, hugging her mother.

"Robin," Mr. Carter scolded. "What in the world would make you call your mother an applehead?"

"You were an applehead too, Dad," Andy informed him. "Robin and I saved you!"

"Owen, the scarecrow, helped us," Robin added.

"What are you two talking about?" Mrs. Carter asked.

Robin and Andy started from the beginning. They didn't leave out a single detail. But their parents didn't believe a word.

"You guys are too much." Mr. Carter chuckled. "You

were complaining when we got here," he said. "And now you're making up scary stories about the place."

"We're not making them up!" Andy insisted.

Their parents shot each other amused looks.

"Well, I'm glad you two had such a good time," Mr. Carter said. "But I think it's time to go now."

"Home?" Robin asked hopefully.

"No," Mrs. Carter answered, looking at her watch. "It's still early enough to catch one last sight."

Robin and Andy groaned. They were exhausted. The last thing they wanted to do was see more historical sights.

"Come on," Mr. Carter said, heading for the car. "Let's get a move on."

"We'll be right there," Robin told him. "As soon as we say good-bye to Owen."

Owen was standing under the giant shade tree holding Yaga in his hands.

"They don't even know they were appleheads," Andy told Owen.

"I told you," Owen said.

Robin looked around the orchard at all the adults who had been appleheads. Now they were surrounded by the kids who had been zombies. They were all laughing and talking like nothing had happened. "They really don't remember anything, do they?" she asked Owen.

"Nope," Owen said. "But we do." He gave them a wink.

"What about her?" Andy asked, pointing to shriveled-up Yaga.

"She's harmless now," Owen said. "This rotten old

applehead will never bother anybody ever again."

"What about you?" Robin asked.

Owen shrugged. "I'm not sure," he said. "But I still have the heart of a young person, so I think I've got some good years left in me. I think I'll stay right here and run the orchard," Owen decided. "The right way. Maybe you two can even come help me once in a while."

Robin smiled. "You bet," she said.

"Yeah," Andy agreed. "That'll be fun."

Just then their father blew the car horn. "Kids!" he called. "Let's go!"

"We'll see you around, Owen," Robin said as she and Andy headed for the car.

"Guess what we're going to see next?" their mother asked a few minutes later.

Mr. Carter turned down the bumpiest road Robin had ever been on.

"What?" Robin asked, afraid to hear the answer.

"Appleton Lagoon," their mother informed them. "It sounds pretty neat. Listen to what the guidebook says."

Robin and Andy shot each other worried looks.

Their mother started to read. "'Legend has it that Appleton Lagoon is home to the biggest sea serpent in the world, even bigger than the Loch Ness Monster,'"

"Who knows?" Mr. Carter chuckled. "Maybe we'll spot him."

Robin hoped not.

"Oh, look," her mother said, pointing up ahead. "There it is."

As the car turned onto the road that led to the lagoon, Robin and Andy had to laugh. Appleton Lagoon looked more like a small lake than the home of a giant sea serpent.

"Come on, kids," Mrs. Carter said, climbing out of the car. "This is going to be fun."

Robin and Andy followed their parents to the lagoon. Based on what she now knew of Appleton's history, Robin wasn't sure what to expect. But luckily, there wasn't anything to see but a lot of dirty, murky lagoon water.

"Boy, Mom," Robin grumbled. "This was really great."

"Yeah," Andy agreed. "Now let's go home."

Just then their father spotted a nest of birds up in an oak tree. "Oh, look, honey," he said, pointing up. "There's a robins' nest up there."

"Where?" Mrs. Carter struggled to see.

"Come around here," Mr. Carter said, moving behind the tree. "You'll be able to see better."

Robin and Andy rolled their eyes at each other.

"Terrific," Andy huffed. "Now we're going to be here all day looking at birds."

But Andy was wrong.

Robin saw the water in the lagoon start to part. Something big rose straight up from the center.

Andy gasped when he saw it too—an enormous green sea monster with two pointed fangs.

"Uh, Mom?" Robin could barely choke the words out. "We've got a problem here!"

"We'll be with you in just one second, Robin," her mother called from under the oak tree.

"We don't have one second!" Robin cried.

The sea serpent stretched out its long, giant neck. Before Robin could even scream, it opened its mouth, ready to swallow up the oak tree . . . and the two goofy parents standing under it.

Get ready for more . . .

Here's a preview of the next spine-chilling book
from A. G. Cascone

ALONG CAME A SPIDER

The dusty old science kit under Mikey's bed is full of creepy,
crawly, disgusting creatures. But they're all in jars, all long
dead. At least, they're supposed to be. But when Mikey and
his best friend, Max, open the jar with the man-eating
spider inside, they're in for the shock of their lives. The
spider's alive! And it's running loose in Mikey's house . . .

Mikey was about to say something when the most horrifying sound cut through the air.

Yeeeeee-oooooowwwwww! Raaaaarrrrrreeee! It was like nothing Mikey had ever heard before. It was loud and ferocious, almost unearthly, and it was coming from the foyer.

"What the heck is that?" Max gasped.

Mikey's heart stopped, but the sound didn't.

"You don't think it's the spider, do you?" Max asked nervously.

"Spiders don't growl," Mikey shot back. At least he hoped not.

Another loud, wailing yowl tore through the house.

"Uh-oh," Mikey said. "I think it's Fluffy."

Max swallowed hard. "Do we have to go check on her?"

Mikey nodded. He didn't want to go either. With the way Fluffy was carrying on, who knew what they'd find? He inched his way into the foyer, with Max right behind him.

Fluffy was backed into the corner opposite the stairs. Her back was arched and her fur stood on end, making her look three times her normal size. Her teeth were bared, and she was yowling and hissing, spitting up a storm.

"What's wrong with her?" Max whispered.

Mikey was too horrified to answer. He just pointed.

The black spider stood on the floor in front of Fluffy. *Its* hair was on end too!

Mikey blinked. It wasn't the spider's hair that made it look three times its size. The horrible creature was actually growing!

In less than two minutes flat, the spider had grown from the size of a dime to the size of a Ping-Pong ball!

"Geez, oh man," Max yelped. "He's getting bigger!"

"I know," Mikey cried back.

"How is that possible?" Max asked. "He's supposed to be dead!"

Fluffy let out another wail.

"Get it, you stupid cat!" Mikey screamed at the terrified fur ball.

But the cat didn't move. She didn't even look at Mikey. She just kept her eyes on the spider, yowling all the while.

The spider began creeping toward Fluffy, backing her deeper and deeper into the corner.

"You don't think he can really hurt her, do you, Max?" Mikey asked.

But before Max could say anything, Mikey got his answer.

Fluffy swiped at the spider with her paw. That was a terrible mistake. The spider buried its horrible fangs deep into Fluffy's leg.

Fluffy let out a screech, then shot straight up into the air as if she'd been fired from a cannon. She flew over the spider and raced up the stairs, leaving a trail of blood droplets behind her.

"Did you see that?" Mikey gasped.

"I told you that thing was a man-eater!" Max yelped, backing away.

"Fluffy's a cat, not a man, you moron," Mikey pointed out. He was trying to stay calm. "And the spider didn't exactly eat her either."

"What are you talking about? He just took a huge chunk of flesh out of her leg!" Max jumped in. "If Fluffy hadn't run away, who knows what other body parts that zombie spider would have tried to chow down on!"

Mikey didn't have a chance to respond. The spider had turned around, and now it was coming toward them. . . .

DESERONTO PUBLIC LIBRARY

Collect them all!

About the Author

A. G. Cascone is the pseudonym of two authors. Between them, they have written six previous books, two horror movie screenplays, and several pop songs, including one top-ten hit.

If you want to find out more about DEADTIME STORIES or A. G. Cascone, look on the World Wide Web at:
        http://www.bookwire.com/titles/deadtime/

Also, we'd love to hear from you! You can write to
        A. G. Cascone
        c/o Troll
        100 Corporate Drive
        Mahwah, NJ 07430–1404

Or you can send e-mail directly to:
        agcascone@bookwire.com